Oh
*Ginny*
*Aunt!*

Oh My

Giddy

Aunt!

# Oh My
# Giddy
# Aunt!

## A Relative Problem

## JAY CASSIE

*Illustrations by Garry Davies*

Matador
9 Priory Business Park,
Wistow Road, Kibworth Beauchamp,
Leicestershire. LE8 0RX
Tel: (+44) 116 279 2299
Fax: (+44) 116 279 2277
Email: books@troubador.co.uk
Web: www.troubador.co.uk/matador


ISBN 978 1780883 939

British Library Cataloguing in Publication Data.
A catalogue record for this book is available from the British Library.

Typeset by Troubador Publishing Ltd, Leicester, UK
Printed and bound in Great Britain by
Clays Ltd, St Ives plc

**Matador** is an imprint of Troubador Publishing Ltd

*This book is dedicated to my very special friends.*
*Thank you*

# Preface

Why is it, that we always think other people's eccentric relations are amusing, but when faced with our own, we feel they are millstones around our necks? Like all normal families we had a relative problem — my Great Aunt Lillian.

My mother, who was quite straight-laced, was heard to say on many occasions: "Oh my giddy aunt! Not again. What will the neighbours think?" This always occurred when Auntie had caused some embarrassment in the village.

Villages can be very close knit and gossip can cause trouble.

Aunt Lillian was birdlike in stature, only five feet tall, and she rushed around with the energy of a rampaging five-year-old. Bustling here and there, she would leave a trail of unintentional devastation in her wake, quite oblivious of the chaos and embarrassment she had caused.

My Uncle Arthur was the exact opposite, being a phlegmatic man who took everything in his stride and only felt action was necessary when the whirlwind that he had married disrupted his peaceful view of life. Then he put his foot down with a firm hand and everyone listened.

Most of the time he escaped to the shed down on his allotment and smoked his pipe. This was his escape from the world and he remained blind to some of my aunt's more outrageous escapades. When he left for work each day it must have been in some trepidation, never sure of what he would find upon his return.

The locals treated my aunt like a living soap opera. They laughed at her exploits in the local pub on Sunday mornings, discussed them in the doctor's surgery, on the bus or while waiting in the queue at the bakers. Lillian was always seen as a rich source of entertainment.

They all knew her and some avoided her, but I think most were quite proud of their acquaintance with a true eccentric. Over the years, she provided them with endless stories to entertain their neighbours, dinner guests and relations, but we were the family that had to live with her.

My mother found her a constant irritation and she felt that her life was somewhat blighted by living in the same village as this whirling dervish. If she espied her when out shopping, she would grab my arm and pull me into a shop doorway, just to avoid being seen with her. I think my mother had delusions of grandeur which were crushed when neighbours rushed to inform her of my aunt's latest incident or misdemeanour.

As a child I spent a lot of time with my aunt. I loved her deeply and was secretly proud of the fact that she was not like everyone else. I always looked on her as a role model. I wanted to be like her when I grew up, not become one of those dull fuddy-duddy women who let old age take them over. Lillian would not let Attila the Hun take her over, let alone Old Father Time.

Ninety-one and counting – that was the age she admitted to when she died and I know that in the past she had taken years off, but I suspect, as death approached, she began putting just a few on to enhance her status.

Lillian was always the consummate actress; she could be a she-devil or an aged angel. She switched, like a multi-personality freak, so you were never bored in her company. Shocked sometimes, but never bored.

She frequently talked to God on a one to one basis, just like the little priest Don Camillo in the novels by Giovanni Guareschi, and I know that she informed him how heaven would undergo some changes when she eventually quit this mortal coil and got there to organise things. I feel that God left her with us so long because he could not quite pluck up the courage to gather her to his bosom. Perhaps he hoped that she would, given enough time, commit some major sin so that he could, with a clear conscience, send her down to the opposition. On the other hand, I am not sure that the Devil would have been up to coping with Lillian either.

Most people don't want to stand out from the crowd, but Lillian certainly did. There was no question about it – she was known to the police, the church and the local council.

In our politically correct world she would have been in court on a regular basis for one reason or another, or on the front page of the tabloids. She was not mad, but extremely unconventional, and was known by everyone as Old Mother Auger.

Nowadays she would have been considered eligible for a compulsory place in a care home, but not then. Indeed, under current government guidelines, she could have been declared insane. We would probably have had to have her sectioned, but then she was free to indulge her eccentricities to her heart's content and we kids loved her for it.

Secretly, my friends and, especially myself, were proud of her notoriety – we were somehow famous as a family. My school chums clamoured to be included in her circle and were always ready to join in – perhaps this youthful audience encouraged her to greater feats of exuberance.

She was a constant source of joy to me and I loved spending time with her, especially when sharing in her many exploits and adventures. As a child I never felt a sense of embarrassment, just a warm glow of pride that my aunt threw off the shackles of age and lived life to the full and here are some of her adventures.

## CHAPTER I

# Lazy People Take Most Pains

Would you leave an elderly delinquent in charge of your house and children? No, I didn't think so, but my mother made the great mistake of leaving Aunt Lillian in charge of me and the house when she went off to visit my Gran for a couple of days.

You could say that it was all Mum's fault when things went awry, as they always seemed to when Aunt Lillian had anything to do with it. It was not the first and would certainly not be the last time that disaster struck when she was in charge.

I walked home from school with some trepidation; you never knew what to expect when she had been left alone in the house for any length of time and today was no exception. As I approached, the back door was open and, to my surprise, our garden was covered with soapy water and our ducks were waddling around covered in foam. Our dog Patsy was standing amidst the flood, howling and barking enough to wake the dead and looking very scared and I noticed the net curtains in the house opposite were twitching.

What had she done this time?

As I hurried up the back steps I gave a cheery wave to the nosy neighbour. I hated the way she spied on us kids and wanted to let her know that I had seen her.

It was much worse than I could have imagined and I stopped dead in my tracks surveying a scene of utter chaos. There were islands of soap suds floating around looking like the remnants of an arctic melt down and there was a loud noise coming from the washing machine. It was trying to make its way across the kitchen like a demented Dalek, clanking and clanging as it went. The hose outlet was swinging from side to side like an elephant's trunk disgorging more water onto the floor, the sink was overflowing and Aunt Lillian was nowhere to be seen.

It was then that I noticed our poor cat clambering onto the kitchen table trying valiantly to carry two kittens in her mouth at once. The other four kittens were mewing pathetically awaiting rescue on the stool in front of the Aga.

I waded into the waters of Noah's Flood which lapped up around my ankles, threw my satchel on the table and shouted "Auntie! What have you done this time and where the heck are you?"

Our kitchen is at a lower level and rushing up the two steps into the living room I saw her standing there with large earphones clamped to her head. The sound of the 1812 Overture at full volume vibrated across the room. The assault on Moscow was in full swing and she was conducting the orchestra in a way that could only be described as manic. Sir Malcolm Sargent on speed!

"What happened in the kitchen and where did all the water come from? And why is the washing machine making all that noise?" I screamed.

"What water? What washing machine?"

"This water" pointing down at my wet feet "and that washing machine" I shouted loudly, pointing into the kitchen.

"Oh. I forgot all about that. I thought that the guns were louder than usual but I thought that Napoleon had learned from his past mistakes and had brought in reinforcements this time."

She gave me a smile. "I can explain you know."

"I think that Mum will want some sort of explanation. You should see the mess out there."

"Well," she paused for effect, "you know how much I hate washing up and you know that I was trying to find new ways of making life easier?"

"Yes" I whispered tentatively.

"I was getting a bit bored so I thought I would help your mum whilst I was over here and spring clean the china cabinet. It was looking a bit dusty you know."

"Yeees" I said slowly.

"That was what I did and you will be really impressed."

She carried on with the story as if nothing had happened and the washing machine was still thumping and banging in the background: "When I got all the china out and put it on the table I realised that it was going to be a mammoth job and I would need some extra help so I thought that this was a good opportunity to put my new idea to the test."

I knew of my aunt's ideas. They were trouble with a capital T.

"So you put it in the washing machine?"

"Jojo, do you think I am stupid or something?  I know

about mechanical things you know. I checked it out and the drum does not go round, there is just a little spinner thing in the back so I knew it would be alright. The water would just flow around the dishes carrying away all the dust and grime and they would come out all clean and sparkling."

"Tell me you didn't!" I was really worried by now.

"Didn't what?" she asked sweetly. "Stop worrying. I piled it carefully up round the sides of the drum and put in the washing powder, closed the lid and made sure that I put it on the lowest speed. I then decided to listen to Sir Malcolm whilst the machine did all the work. It was all going so well – all the china washed in one go and I knew that your mother would be really pleased with me for a change, but then......."

In the distance I could hear a siren which seemed to be getting nearer and nearer. Then all of a sudden three firemen rushed in the back door and came to an abrupt halt. We hurried back into the kitchen.

"What happened here?" one of them started to say but then he stopped. "Oh, Mrs Auger, it's you."

"Of course it is me, officer. Who did you expect it to be – Old Mother Slipper Slopper?"

"What is causing all the noise?" he bellowed.

I pointed to the washing machine which had now come to a halt by the back door. He rushed across and quickly switched it off and turned off the taps at the same time. "You could have been electrocuted you silly old woman," he added.

"Don't you call me an old woman," she replied sharply.

I noticed that she did not remonstrate about being called silly.

"Well, you don't live here and when we got the call from one of the neighbours saying that water was pouring out of the house and the dog was barking madly, we expected it to be a real emergency. If we had known you were here we would have taken our time," laughed the second fireman.

"That is not the attitude to take young man. Just because you have been called out before to save me from a disaster that was not my fault, it doesn't mean that it is always a false alarm."

"OK" he sighed. "Now we are here, where did all this water come from?"

"That is none of your business young man. I was just washing the kitchen floor and I got a bit carried away, that's all." She drew herself up to her full five foot and said: "You can go now. Things are completely under control."

He sighed. "Come on lads. Let's leave her to it." The second fireman turned round to me: "Hi Jojo. Are you OK?"

"I think so," I replied.

"We'll go then." He knew there was no point in trying to argue with my aunt. He had tried and failed before and knew when he had met his match.

When they were gone she turned to me and said

gleefully: "I didn't want to say anything when those fellows were here in case they stole my new invention. If it works, I will patent it and make a fortune. Well Jojo, let's look at the results of our handiwork."

"Your handiwork," I retorted. I had been caught up in her schemes before and somehow she always managed to make it seem that it was my fault.

"Don't be pedantic, we'll soon be basking in glory and very rich into the bargain," she said as she made her way over to the washing machine. "Anyway, how did the washing machine get here? It wasn't here when I filled it up."

I didn't bother to reply.

She lifted the lid and I could tell from the look on her face that things had not quite gone according to plan when she asked: "Are you any good at doing jigsaws? We're going to need someone who is really good at doing jigsaws."

"What have jigsaws got to do with anything? But as a matter of fact I am quite good, now that you ask. I completed a one thousand piece one that I got for my birthday and I managed to finish it all by myself. It was really complicated with lots of blue sky."

"I think you are going to need all those skills," she said holding up two large pieces of mother's favorite plate. "Don't worry though; I saw this programme on TV the other day where invisible repairs were made to broken or chipped china. You couldn't even see the join. It will just be a matter of patience and perseverance and we will have it looking as good as new in no time. A bit of 'UHU' glue and no one will know what happened. Anyway the dinner service will not be needed until next Christmas but if your mother notices, I will tell her that the cracks must have been caused by a minor earthquake or the vibration from the heavy traffic going past in the lane."

"We don't have earthquakes here and there is no heavy traffic going past. We live on the quietest lane in the village," I reasoned.

"Don't be difficult Jojo. There were no cracks in the china when I took it out this morning. This must have been caused by something. It can't have been the machine as why would anyone invent a machine that caused such havoc?" She turned and looked at me quite archly when I pointed out that it was meant for clothes and not china.

"Well I know that, but things can be adapted for other uses if you put your mind to it. It's just a matter of application," she muttered. "That is how things get invented."

"But washing machines are not meant for washing up the best china though!" I pointed out.

"Ok clever clogs! So are you just going to stand there like a lemon or are you going to help me stick this all together? We need to get it finished and back in the china cabinet before your mother gets back you know."

Even at my age I realised the futility of trying to 'mend' the china and pointed this out to her.

"It will just take a little bit of time, and your mother doesn't go into the front room very often, so I will put a blanket over the china cabinet and tell her that she needs to keep the sun off it in case it fades. Then we can do a cup and saucer a day when she is not around and move on to the plates and bowls. Patience is the name of the game. We'll have it done in no time at all."

I laughed "No time? It will take years."

"Don't be defeatist. That's the problem with young people these days, no sticking power."

I burst out laughing "We will need more sticking power than the King's men needed to put Humpty Dumpty together again, if we are going to fix this," pointing to the thousands of pieces in the bottom of the drum.

She moved over to the sink and grabbed the kettle. "Let's have a nice cup of tea and a couple of custard creams before you start cleaning up this mess. That will help us think of a solution."

A cup of tea was my aunt's answer to everything and I noticed that she had said that I was going to be clearing up the mess. Luckily we had a drain in the middle of the flagstone floor and the water had already receded somewhat.

The cat was climbing down from the table and gave my aunt a superior look that only a cat can come up with and our dog cautiously pushed open the back door. Animals knew instinctively to avoid her and when to return.

"Well, at least the kitchen floor has had a good wash. Your mother was never that good at cleaning." She took the mugs down from the shelf and reached for the biscuit barrel: "Anyway, I didn't like that service very much. It was quite ugly you know."

"You might not have liked it very much, but it was mum's pride and joy. What is she going to say? She will go loopy you know."

"Don't be silly my dear. She will never notice the difference when we have stuck it together again."

At that moment she noticed that our ducks had come into the kitchen and Patsy was trying her best to slink under the table: "What is the matter with that dog and why is it so wet? I think you had better shoo the ducks out into the garden. You know your mother hates them coming in the house. What is this world coming to?"

At that moment the kettle started to whistle cheerily and I went to my bedroom to change out of my school uniform. Upon returning to the kitchen I went to the cupboard to get the mop and bucket to start the clear up. My aunt always did have a short term memory problem when it came to remembering disasters of her own making and I knew there was no point in trying to reason with her when she had her mind set on something.

It was just another day in the life of my crazy Aunt.

CHAPTER 2

# A Spoonful of Medicine

The problem started when Aunt Lillian decided to become an amateur vet. My giddy aunt felt that she was ideally qualified to cut the claws of her cat Tarzan and her dog Pegotty. But, like so many of her ideas, this latest brainwave backfired on her.

Cutting the cat's claws had ended with Aunt Lillian having to go to the cottage hospital to be given a tetanus jab! She had forgotten to bind Tarzan up tightly in a towel before going mad with the nail clippers. The cat had fought back with great vigour, and certainly lived up to his name. Indeed, he had won the battle fair and square – no question about it!

Clipping the dog had subsequently needed a visit to the local dog groomer to sort out the poor animal before it died of embarrassment. Dogs hate to be laughed at and trying to create a poodle from a mongrel had caused distress. Pompoms protecting the joints ended up being just tufts of hair and a bare midriff did nothing for Pegotty's image. The poor animal looked a sight for weeks as she slunk around the garden trying not to be noticed.

So it was with some unease that I entered the kitchen to be greeted with: "Hi, Jojo. My dear little Alfie looks proper poorly and I think he needs a tonic."

Alfie was her goldfish and he had always looked quite perky to me. "What do you think is the matter with him?" I asked.

"He is just ignoring that new arch that I created for him," she said, pointing to the hideous multi-coloured creation that stood in the bottom of a very crowded fish tank. "I spent all day yesterday painting it and I thought he would really be pleased, but he did not seem at all grateful. I don't want him getting bored. Animals need diversions to keep them active and healthy."

I took a closer look in the tank and offered my opinion. "Alfie is a fish – not an animal – and I don't think he requires all those playthings that you have put in there. He can hardly move. He needs space to swim around and get some exercise; otherwise he will get really fat."

But Aunt Lillian was adamant. "No," she insisted, "what he needs is a tonic – and I have just the thing." She reached into the cupboard under the sink and pulled out a large bottle with no label on it. "Give me a small teaspoon from that drawer," she instructed.

Belying her years and her tiny five foot frame, Aunt Lillian pulled the fish tank towards her and reached in it, up to her elbow. Alfie sensibly swam into the corner behind the Eiffel Tower and warily looked out through the weeds.

"Come here, Alfie" she called, "there is nothing to be frightened of. Mummy just wants to make you feel better."

I suspect that Alfie had seen what happened to the other pets when 'mummy' wanted to make them feel better and he kept his distance.

Aunt Lillian proceeded to chase him around the tank before she shouted: "Come here, you little devil. I will give you what for when I do catch you."

Alfie was not giving in easily. He swooped under the new arch and my aunt took the skin off her knuckles as she tried to grab him.

"Oh sugar!!" This was Aunt Lillian's latest swear word.

"You had better not let Mum hear you say that," I scolded. "I got a smack when I said it the other day and Michael was sent to bed with no tea for shouting 'blugger'. Mum said that we had thought a bad word, even if we had not actually said it."

"Your mother has no sense of humour — that's her trouble," Aunt Lillian confided, wiping the blood from her fingers on the tea towel. "Hand me that sieve will you? I can't let Alfie get away with it. If I do, he will think he is the boss — training always starts with establishing who is top dog."

Alfie was swimming along the front of the tank and looked as though he was gloating.

"I think he is top dog at the moment as he drew first blood," I pointed out.

Aunt Lillian took the sieve and came up quickly

behind him. "Ha, caught you. You didn't get away that time." She turned to me. "Pour a bit out of the bottle into the spoon and hand it to me carefully."

I picked up the bottle and took the top off.

"What is this?" I asked, sniffing at it. "Urgh! It's cod liver oil. You can't give that to Alfie. It will kill him."

"I'll have you know that I give cod liver oil to all my pets when they are under the weather."

I already knew this as I had often been overwhelmed by the fishy breath of her cats and dogs.

Peggotty was her devoted and long suffering companion. She was a strangely shaped dog, somewhat like a triangle – very wide at the back, tapering to a point at the front. At the local dog sanctuary she had been rejected by everyone because of her strange appearance – until my aunt took pity on her.

"Hurry up, Jojo. Alfie is gasping for breath. Hand me the spoon."

"Won't this make Alfie into a cannibal?" I inquired. "After all, it is made from fish."

She paused: "I hadn't thought of that. Never mind, it's made from cod liver and not gold fish. So it will be all right," and with that she poured the contents of the spoon into the gaping mouth of the fish.

Alfie coughed, wriggled and then coughed again. Finally he lay still and his eyes glazed over.

"What's the matter with him?" cried Aunt Lillian, peering at him through her tiny National Health glasses.

"I think you have drowned him," I replied.

Aunt Lillian was unrepentant. "Don't be silly. You can't drown a fish — they are used to swimming in water and anyway, they breathe through their gills not their mouths."

I tried to reason with her. "Swimming in water is one thing, but having a teaspoonful of cod liver oil forced down his throat was quite another."

She laid him down on the tea towel but he did not move.

"Perhaps I should give him some artificial respiration. I learnt about that when I did a first aid course. That should do the trick." She proceeded to gently push on his chest. Nothing happened.

"Mouth to mouth resuscitation will bring him round!" she exclaimed, grabbing the poor gold fish and starting to blow into his mouth — again nothing.

He was a very small fish, but I had visions of him blowing up like a giant gold balloon and floating up to the ceiling.

"It's no use — he's dead. You've killed him, Auntie," I said sorrowfully. "I think he would have got used to the arch and would have enjoyed swimming under it if he had been given half a chance."

Finally Aunt Lillian began to feel guilty. "Poor Alfie — I didn't mean to do that to you." She looked down at him sadly and then brightened up. "Perhaps he is just pretending to be dead to make me feel bad. He is quite a joker you know."

She needed a reality check and it was up to me to give it to her. "Auntie," I said. "You chased him until he was exhausted, dragged him out of his tank, choked him and blew him up. How can you possibly doubt that he's dead? And if by some miracle he was still alive, he'd hardly be in the mood for joking."

"I really loved him, you know," Auntie muttered. "I just wanted to make him feel better." She wiped her eyes on her apron and declared: "Anyway, what is done is done and there is no point in crying over spilt cod liver oil, so hand me that Swan Vesta match box from over by the cooker. We can put him in there and bury him in the garden."

I looked out of the window. "It's pouring with rain. We'll get soaked."

"Then we will just have to wait. So put the kettle on Jojo, but leave the match box open. I am sure poor Alfie was frightened of the dark because he used to swim round and round frantically when I put the light out each evening."

We sat down at the kitchen table with our mugs of tea, looking at the head of the fish peeping out of the matchbox.

"I know what we will do. We don't want to get soaked." Aunt Lillian jumped up and ran into the bedroom. After a few minutes she emerged, dressed in black and carrying a black lace shawl.

She went over to the gramophone player and put on the record of Handel's 'Dead March' from Saul which blared out into the kitchen at full volume. This was one of her favourites and was kept on the gramophone for times of distress or disaster.

"We will have a funeral service and sing a hymn or two," she shouted, throwing the shawl at me.

"Come on, get yourself ready. We have to show some respect for Alfie, even if he was only a fish."

I didn't have the heart to tell my aunt that she had shown little respect for him earlier. So I confined myself to saying: "Okay, I'll get my mackintosh and wellingtons."

"You don't need a coat. We will stay here in the warm," she told me.

"How will we be able to have a funeral service if we don't go outside?"

"Do you know, the trouble with you is that you have no imagination?" Aunt Lillian chided. "Come with me – I know exactly what to do." She closed the matchbox with a flourish and led the way down the hall, turning left into the toilet.

It was a bit of a tight squeeze. "We will just flush him down the loo," she announced. "That way we will not have to go outside in the wet and he will be able to join other fish in the sea. It is a much better way for a fish to end his days than being buried in the cold, dark ground."

She carefully placed the matchbox in the toilet and started: "Dust to dust and ashes to... " Here she stopped. "That doesn't sound right. Let me think for a moment: How about this?" She then started to declaim in her best

Sunday voice: "Fish to water and water to sea, in the hope of resurrection in the big pond in the sky." With that, she pulled the chain.

After the first rush of water subsided there was Alfie in his little coffin floating above the waterline.

"I forgot that the matchbox would float," said Aunt Lillian. She grabbed the offending box, extracted Alfie, laid him back in the water and again pulled the chain.

We both held our breath, but when we looked down, the little fish was still bobbing up and down in the pan. My aunt yanked at the chain, almost pulling it off the cistern. After seven attempts she had to admit defeat. So she put Alfie back into the wet matchbox and handed him to me.

"There is nothing for it, Jojo – you will just have to get your sou'wester and wellingtons and do the job properly. Don't forget to put him with the other fish I've buried as I am hoping to plant a row of seed potatoes there and fish bone meal helps produce a really good crop of King Edwards."

I had to smile. My Aunt Lillian had an answer for everything.

# CHAPTER 3

# Revenge on the Bankers

Unlike most couples in those days, my aunt and uncle had separate bank accounts – in fact, they used different banks. That was the cause of the trouble really.

Aunt Lillian banked with Martins – she had chosen it because it was the one with the grasshopper sign above the door, which appealed to her sense of fun. My uncle used the services of the National Provincial. The banks stood opposite one another in the High Street, and money was transferred into my aunt's account without fail each week for the housekeeping.

One morning she announced to me: "It is eleven o'clock and I must go into the bank to get some money before we go shopping." At times she could be very precise and woe betide the assistant who did not have her money ready for her at 11a.m. sharp.

She was well known in Martins as being an 'awkward' customer and I noticed that when she entered, all the bank tellers tried to look busy, presumably hoping she would not choose to deal with them. This was not going to work as the bank was empty, so she was able to take her pick –

until two of the four cashiers promptly left their posts!

An unfortunate young man with a thin face and acute acne became today's 'victim'. She marched up to his counter and demanded: "Well, are you going to serve me or just sit there looking into space?"

I always imagined that the tellers drew lots as to who would serve her each week, for there was nearly always some problem or altercation.

"Oh, Mrs Auger, I did not see you there," the poor chap squeaked.

"Are you blind or something?" she asked. "Perhaps you need glasses, but now I have your attention, I would like my usual withdrawal if that is not too much trouble young man." She thrust a withdrawal slip under the bars and waited.

After a few minutes I noticed that the young man was going rather red in the face and wriggling about like a fish on a hook. "Err, I am sorry Mrs Auger," he began "but you do not seem to have sufficient funds to cover this."

"What are you talking about, I must have," she snapped. "My husband's bank sends money to you every week without fail and I come in here and collect it each Friday. If you have not got the money: then who has got it?"

She was getting quite agitated. "Who's been stealing my money? I want to see the manager immediately," she shouted. "Security in this establishment leaves a lot to be desired when a poor old lady is robbed right under your noses."

"There must be some explanation," I said, frantically pulling at her sleeve.

"I don't need an explanation – I need my money and I need it right now." She was beginning to raise her voice and the teller cowered down under the tirade.

"Well, don't just sit there like a stuffed rabbit," Aunt Lillian demanded. "Get someone to find my money. I don't have all day to stand around here waiting you know."

"I… I… I'll go and get the manager," he stammered.

"I should think so, too – not before time I must say." Turning to me my aunt said: "Jojo, do not use this bank to keep your savings in, they are inefficient if they let people just help themselves to other people's money."

By now other customers had arrived and were watching with mild amusement how this fragile, grey-haired old lady was dictating to bank staff. I could see that they were waiting for the main event which was sure to follow.

Suddenly a side door opened and out stepped the bank manager Mr. Groves. "I hear there is a little problem with your account, Mrs Auger."

"There is no problem with my account, but there is a problem with your bank," she retorted. "You have allowed someone to take money from my account. So what are you going to do about it?"

"I have a copy of your account here," the portly Mr. Groves said calmly, waving a piece of paper under her nose, "and the balance is not sufficient to cover the withdrawal you wish to make. We didn't receive the usual deposit of funds. Unless you would like to arrange an overdraft, there is nothing that I can do about it."

"We'll see about that," Aunt Lillian snapped. "I am going to National Provincial over the road to find out what has happened, but I will return. I need money to buy the Sunday joint and some other bits and bobs and I am in a hurry. Come on, Jojo, we'll go and find out what the problem really is. We can't expect these nincompoops to sort this out."

With that she turned on her heel and, dragging me after her, exited the bank with a flourish.

Somehow Aunt Lillian saw banks as a money repository in the old fashioned sense of the word. In her mind the bright, modern area that the customers saw was a front, a 'fake' presented to give people confidence in the banking system.

She had told me in the past, that behind the scenes there were dimly lit rooms full of bags of coins and gold bars; stacks of bank notes were pawed over by clerks wearing visors with pencils tucked behind their ears, counting and checking by day and night. They had their shirt sleeves held up with elastic round their upper arms and they entered their findings in large ledgers using quill pens. She actually seemed to believe that they sat on high stools, behind rows of desks and were watched over by a Scrooge-like character. She imagined them to be brow beaten Bob Cratchits, blowing on their hands to warm themselves because there was no coal to put on the open fire.

I suggested to Aunt Lillian that we went home and borrowed some money from Mum. She peered at me above her glasses as if she was a teacher addressing a petulant pupil and said: "No, Jojo, I fell out with your mother last week over money and she wouldn't lend me a penny now. She would rather see me starving and sent to the workhouse. Come on, we are going to find out what has happened to my money."

"Of course Mum will lend you the money. She was just a bit annoyed when you accused her of being a miser when she refused to lend you money to buy that hat you wanted. She will have forgotten all about it by now and will understand that you need money for housekeeping. Anyway, Uncle Arthur will be home later and then you can come shopping tomorrow."

However, there was no reasoning with her when she had her mind set on a course of action. Entering the bank opposite had much the same effect on the staff there – they had dealt with her before. She clearly did not understand the modern banking system and was too impatient to have it explained to her.

When we got to the front of the queue she asked: "Which of you has got my money and why have you not taken it over to my bank across the road?"

At that moment the bank manager, a balding Welshman called Mr. Morgan just happened to be coming out of his office. She espied him and shouted his name loudly. He stopped and cringed slightly, but turned with a bright smile: "Ah, Mrs Auger, how are you this bright morning? I so hope that you are well."

"I don't know why you are so cheerful when your bank is in such a mess," she said abruptly. "I need my money and that bank over the road tells me they don't have it, so you must have it here. I would be grateful if you could arrange for it to be taken over to Martins immediately so that I can get it out. I have chores to do and no time to stand around here all day."

He patiently explained: "In this modern day and age, money is transferred electronically and I will arrange for one of my staff to see what the problem is."

"You don't need to speak to one of your staff. I need you to get my money and take it across the road so that I can do my shopping," she persisted. "I don't want electronic money – I want cash. My husband uses this bank and sends me money each Friday."

Mr. Morgan knew he was beaten and, with a sigh, informed us: "I will go and see what the problem is."

Five minutes later he returned, apologising for a slight error that had been made. He explained that the usual transfer had not gone through on time and once again tried to talk my aunt through the procedures, but to no avail.

I felt so sorry for Mr. Morgan, who now had a trickle of sweat running down the side of his cheek. He finally gave in, went behind the counter and took out £20 in notes.

Then, escorted by Aunt Lillian and myself, he walked across the road to the rival bank and handed the money to the teller with the spotty face. Mr. Morgan explained that this was the money which should have been transferred, but due to an oversight had been missed, and asked if it could be credited to Mrs Auger's account.

Within seconds the transaction had been made and my aunt had the cash.

"Thank you Mr. Morgan," said Aunt Lillian triumphantly. "Now that wasn't so difficult, was it? Come, Jojo we can now get on with our errands."

Aunt Lillian showed her delight with the outcome, by informing a relieved Mr. Morgan and the harassed young teller in a loud voice: "Thank you both so much for your help, and I compliment you on the level of service you have given today. You should both get a rise." With that, she swept out of the door, clutching her £20.

Turning to me she said: "I have finally got my money. I wasn't going to let them fob me off with electronic money."

I knew that there was no point in arguing with my aunt as, despite her ignorance of the banking system, she had won the day by turning a busy bank manager into her personal courier.

CHAPTER 4

# There Really are Fairies at the Bottom of the Garden

Was she really a witch? As a small child I was convinced my Great Aunt Lillian possessed magical powers. She had a large black cat called Beetle, who she told me was her 'familiar' and she spun the most extraordinary tales of magic and mystery. I would not have been at all surprised if I had seen her flying on a broomstick when the moon was full; wearing a long pointed hat and a flowing cloak covered in arcane symbols of witchcraft billowing out behind her.

She would take me out into the garden to a special part of the lawn, under the chestnut trees, and show me the fairy rings in the grass. Then the stories would begin and today was no exception.

"Come, Jojo. Let's go and find some fairies," whispered 'the witch', alias my Aunt Lillian.

It was a beautiful morning when we ventured down the path. Suddenly she grabbed my sleeve. "Look, here are their ballgowns hanging out to dry. They must have been out to a party last night."

Following her gaze, I saw four spiders' webs, covered with dew, sparkling in the morning sun and dancing in the breeze.

"Those dresses are made of gossamer and you can see the diamonds that have been sewn on them," she went on. "They use these tiny primrose petals," she added, pointing to the ones by her feet, "or those pale white and pink aconites and then they steal the webs of the spider to put over them so that they shimmer in the light of the glow-worms that have to stand around the ballroom."

"Aren't the glow-worms allowed to dance?" I asked, feeling quite sorry for them.

"Oh, no – they just have to stand there for the whole evening, just giving off light."

"That sounds a very boring job," I said, sorrowfully. "And don't the spiders get annoyed if the fairies always steal the webs when they have completed them."

"Sometimes they forget to pay them and then there is trouble," my aunt conceded. "The Queen of the Fairies has to pay a fine to the spinners, but at other times they invite the spiders to join in the festivities. They ride on their backs, like horses, so that they arrive in plenty of time and don't miss any of the dances. Can you imagine what that must be like?"

"Do they have food and drink at their parties?" I wondered.

"They drink nectar from the flowers and eat tiny cakes

made of spun sugar before they go off to dance until dawn," Aunt Lillian replied.

"I wish I could go to one of their balls," I said wistfully.

"Well, perhaps you can if you are very good."

I tried to imagine how splendid it would be. "I could be like Cinderella and have a ballgown made of blue satin, with little glass slippers and a beautiful carriage made out of a pumpkin," I mused.

"Be careful what you wish for Jojo because you would have to shrink down to their size and perhaps you would never be able to come back to the real world."

"I don't care," I insisted. "I could live with them forever and dance until the end of time."

"Hush child, you never know who is listening," my aunt said, looking around her. "You have to be very careful in this garden as it has magical powers all of its own. If you listen carefully you may be able to hear the little folk. This is an enchanted garden."

Yes, I could almost hear the fairies discussing the night's exploits and adventures they had had when we were all fast asleep.

We sat down on the grass together. My aunt lifted her hand to shield her eyes from the sun that had been reflecting off her glasses, while I shut mine as I began to daydream, letting her stories flood over me.

How I loved to look under the flowers to see if I could find just one of the tiny fairies sleeping away the daylight hours. I knew they had tiny beds, made of thistle down, and the caterpillars had been tasked to spin little silken sheets. I would dream of how wonderful it would be to sleep on a bed of soft down, covered with those silken sheets.

Aunt Lillian had told me that the fairies' children slept in tiny cradles, made from pink sea shells, which gently rocked them to sleep. We had some of these shells in the garden that my aunt had brought back from her travels, and she would show me the mother of pearl coverlets which kept their little charges safe and snug at night.

We would search for the acorn cups that were the caps worn by the elves. They were 'de rigueur' for the fashionable elf about town. We would look for the brightest green leaves on the laurel bushes, from which they would make their outfits and my aunt would show me where they would pick buttercups. The petals of these were used by the elves as collars, and I can still picture them in their green and yellow suits, running and hiding from us. I could almost imagine them laughing at us behind our backs and hiding from view. We were always too slow to see them, but I knew they were there.

Aunt Lillian would explain the use of teasels, which grew in great numbers in her garden. These were used by foxes to brush their tails. Ours were the smartest foxes in the village. I knew this was true because I could hear them calling at night. They were telling each other where the best brushes could be found.

I would lie beneath the covers and imagine them

sitting under the full moon, brushing out the tangles in their bushy tails, before they set off to hunt for supper. I would shiver with delight at the secrets that I knew.

Sometimes we would find a fairy ring and dance inside it in our bare feet. Aunt Lillian would chant in a secret language which she said the little people would understand. She promised to give me the magic spells that had been handed down to her as we danced and I was always fascinated by the darker ring of lush grass that grew with the tiny toadstools.

My elderly companion would tell me that if we did not show the proper respect for the tiny people they would turn us into toads – or cause nasty warts to grow on our noses.

Some years later I did get a wart on my hand and realised that I must have passed by a fairy ring without paying my respects. I am more careful now.

Autumn offered the opportunity to discover a new fairy wardrobe filled with red, gold and yellow leaves in which our visitors could clothe themselves while hiding in the woodland.

Fairy milliners would make blackberries into jaunty Russian hats, or turn tiny pieces of beech mast into fashionable sou'westers. Colourful maple leaves were turned into smart jackets and gloves were fashioned from beetle wings which shimmered in the light of the dying sun.

Winter brought dainty snowflakes tumbling down to earth and these they used to create beautiful cloaks, trimmed with the finest down from feathers and lined with the soft white fur of the rabbits, who willingly gave some up to the elfin tailors.

The magic spell surrounding our garden prevented the snowflakes from melting and the fairy kingdom was aglow with tiny lanterns that caught the ice particles and made everything glisten in the moonlight.

With the coming of spring, we would search out the first violets and primroses and Aunt Lillian would tell me of the joy that the little folk felt as they awaited them. New designs for dresses had been in their minds for the whole winter and lily-of-the-valley were gathered to make fashionable hats, or delicate pale blue harebells would be harvested for summer dresses.

My aunt's garden was a wonderland which was brought to life by her enchanting stories, and I still feel a shiver of excitement when I glimpse something that reminds me of her delightful world of make believe that never failed to captivate my imagination.

She once told me that the freckles that covered my nose, of which I was ashamed, were a very special gift from the fairies. They had sprinkled magic dust over me when I was a tiny baby sleeping in my crib and I should be very proud of them.

But sometimes I can't help a little niggling question creeping into my head: was my aunt a witch? No, that would be ridiculous. But there are kind witches, aren't there?

# CHAPTER 5

# The Ton Up Queen

Some people never learn and my cousin Trevor was no exception. He had sold his soul for the money to repair his beloved motorcycle and now he had to pay the price. Aunt Lillian always exacted sweet revenge on people who broke their promises and he knew it. Today was the day when he would have to deliver and so he girded up his loins and decided to get it over with. I could not be expected to miss this confrontation and so I was round at her house bright and early.

"That scamp of a cousin of yours is going to take me out today without fail and I am really going to enjoy it. He has been putting it off for ages and everyone knows that promises must be kept," she chortled.

"I thought promises were meant to be broken," I muttered.

"Oh no – we shook hands on the deal and spat on them to seal it good and tight. He can't renege now, as it is like a sacred pledge."

Just then the sound of the motorbike coming up the drive made her jump up and down like a small child.

"Do you really think this is a good idea?" I asked tentatively. "You are nearly eighty you know and you have never done it before."

"What's that got to do with anything? You are never too old to learn or to have new experiences and I am up for any challenge that life can throw at me. I survived the doodlebugs and buzz bombs that Hitler sent over to wipe me out, I'll have you know."

At that moment the door burst open and Trevor came

in, carrying a black plastic sack which he threw down on the kitchen table: "You will have to wear these as it is against the law not to. I borrowed them from my friend Wilf. If you refuse, then we will have to call the whole thing off," he panted.

Aunt Lillian rushed over to the sack and pulled out the contents. Picking up the leather jacket she shouted: "I just love this logo on the back. It's just me."

She turned it round to display a roaring tiger showing all its teeth and holding the garment up to herself she declared: "Perfect, it will fit like a glove, you'll see." It came down past her knees and almost brushed the tops of her home-made Noddy boot slippers which had silver bells on the toes. She really did have an eclectic taste in fashion.

Then out came the trousers which must have been made with a giant in mind, certainly not her diminutive figure which measured five foot at most.

She threw herself down on the mat with great enthusiasm and tried to pull the trousers on. They concertinaed up around her legs and with difficulty she managed to get her tiny size two feet sticking out the bottom. The trouble was when she let go they reverted to their original length.

Trevor and I looked at one another. "They were the only ones I could get hold of. Wilf is quite tall I suppose and she is very short you know."

"Who are you calling short?" she snapped.

We each took one of Aunt Lillian's arms when her feet

again appeared and quickly stood her up. She looked like a Michelin man with her legs akimbo almost as though she was the kid on the Thelwell pony. She looked a bit red in the face after all the exertion but valiantly declared: "I am sure they will be fine once I get aboard. Hand me that jacket."

We could not resist going along with the charade and helped her into it. Again we realised that she was no Arnold Schwarzenegger, the arms were too long and the tiger sat astride her bottom. She wriggled her hands out of the sleeves and drew herself up to her full height.

At that point she had tripped over and landed in a heap on the floor and the leathers reverted to their original size.

Not to be beaten, she fought with the suit and exclaimed: "How's that? Fits like a glove, as though they were made for me, but I think I will give these trousers a miss."

When he had stopped laughing, Trevor picked up the bright yellow helmet: "Try this for size. We always tease Wilf saying that he has a head like a peanut, so it should fit you."

"Are you insinuating that I have a head like a peanut young man? I will have you know that my head has been admired by many a hairdresser. They told me it was a perfect shape," she retorted, "give it to me."

She put it on her head and it came down over her eyes and enveloped her ears when she tightened the strap. She looked like a turtle as she pushed it up and peered out from under the brim: "It just needs some newspaper in the top and it will be fine. You need to be inventive in situations like these. What are you both laughing at?"

I wiped my eyes and informed her: "You look amazing. Nobody will recognise you in that outfit."

"That is what I am hoping," mumbled Trevor. "Mum will kill me if she finds out about this. She did not want me to have a motorbike in the first place and this will just add fuel to the fire."

"Are you going to tell her? I know Jojo can keep a secret so how is she going to find out?"

"I think the village will tell her when they catch sight of you," I said.

"We will just have to slip through the village like an invisible phantom and then when we get on the motorway we will be doing a hundredweight and will be just a blur on the horizon."

"It's a ton up, not a hundredweight," I giggled.

"Well, let's hit the road and burn some rubber!" she shouted. She was struggling towards the back door with her arms sticking out from her body and the helmet moving from side to side.

She looked quite a sight I can tell you. She looked like an overblown Telly Tubby.

Trevor looked really worried. "I wish I had never made that promise. I know I am going to live to regret it," he whispered.

"Everything will be OK," I said brightly. "After this you will be off the hook and it will teach you never to make a pact with her. It is worse than making it with the Devil. You should know that by now."

Aunt Lillian was attempting to get on the bike, but her short legs were making this difficult.

"You need a mounting block – I will get a box for you to stand on," I said, running to the shed to grab an orange box.

Trevor was now astride his beloved machine and she was mounted up behind him peering round his shoulder.

"Well, what are you waiting for?"

"Are you sure you want to do this? It's not too late to change your mind you know," he said hopefully.

"Just get on with it."

I could see that she was beginning to get annoyed with all the prevarications. "You said you would give me a ride when you had done all the repairs which, incidentally, I seem to have paid for. So I am using my bit of this bike and now it is payback time."

As they sailed down towards the gate I realised that I might miss the fun so I ran after them and took a short cut across the green towards the church which brought me out by the mill. I could hear them as they flew down the High Street. Faster and faster they went; heads were turning and people were pointing. Past the baker, where the Vicar and his wife were just turning into the door, past the post office that was just closing for lunch and on by the people waiting at the bus stop. My aunt was in her element, she was the centre of attention, when she suddenly realised that her skirt was blowing up and she was showing her pink drawers. These were the long pink silky ones, often called passion killers or apple gatherers, that ladies wore then and they came down to the knees held there by elastic. Much as she tried, she could not push her skirt down without letting go of her hold on Trevor's waist.

Everyone turned to stare. The newspaper boy fell off his bike scattering papers in his wake and the local window cleaner spilled water over a passing pedestrian causing her to shout at him.

Havoc ensued as a shopper walked into the barrow where the man was piling up his display of oranges – these scattered into the gutter much to the delight of the local children who ran after them whilst his attention was diverted.

The two dogs that usually sat sunning themselves outside the library decided to give chase barking loudly and all the while adding to the confusion.

The publican ran out of the Rising Sun to see what was happening and nearly fell into the open cellar where the dray man was delivering beer and just saved himself from a nasty fall by grabbing at a barrel which overturned and ran down the road.

It was a catastrophe and mayhem reigned, but I am sure she thought to herself, who cares, they have always thought I was a bit odd, so now they know I am. It will give them all something to talk about.

However, disaster loomed on the horizon, because as Trevor took the bend by the mill pond a car was backing out of the butcher's on the bridge and he had to take quick evasive action, veering onto the wrong side of the road and onto the slippery path that led through the stream.

There was a loud *crash, bang* and the bike skidded down the bank and into the water. The ducks, which up until that point had been swimming around minding their own business, flew up squawking loudly.

I ran to the railing and looked over expecting to see bodies strewn over the mill pond.

They had landed in the reeds that encircled the water and luckily neither of them was hurt and Aunt Lillian looked so comical with the weeds draped around the helmet. The jacket had returned to its original size and acted as a life jacket so she floated rather sedately on the surface.

She was spitting a jet of water but managed to shout: "What did you do that for? Don't think that means you are getting out of keeping your promise. We will give it another go when I get dried off. Now help me up this minute."

At that moment she looked up and saw the crowd gathered on the bridge. "What are all those people staring at?" she asked.

What could poor Trevor say!

She was again the subject of much gossip in the village, but poor Trevor got all the blame for taking a 'poor innocent old lady' on such a dangerous machine.

Life was not fair for anyone who dealt with Aunt Lillian.

# CHAPTER 6

# The Dog's Got Fleas!

My Aunt Lillian was in full cry and there was no stopping her. "The dog's got fleas – and that has given me an idea on how to get my own back on Mrs Garton and her village fete!" she exclaimed. "Ban me from attending, would she!"

She continued without pausing for breath. "It's at the top of my list of things to do," she said, shaking a piece of paper under my nose.

This was her opening gambit when I arrived at her cottage just a week before the annual village fete was due to take place. Competition had always been rife between my aunt and the ladies of the WVS and WI, who worked in tandem to run the Golden Acre Summer Fete, so I feared that out and out war had now been declared.

"Now we will see who can draw in the crowds," she went on before I could reply. "We are going to set up an alternative show that will knock the socks off her wishy-washy event. So there, what do you think about that, Jojo?"

Before I could tell her, she thrust a rickety cardboard

model under my nose and instructed: "Look at this! It will be the main attraction."

At last I managed to get a word in. "What is it?" I enquired. It did not look like much of anything. A cut down cardboard box, stuck together with sticking plaster, housed what I could only deduce was supposed to be a see-saw and a hamster wheel.

"Golden Acre will be empty as all the village will be queuing at that front gate," my aunt declared, pointing out of the window. "We will sell advance tickets to avoid a riot, as I do not want to make the headlines in the local paper again. Once was enough and your mother never lets me forget it."

Golden Acre was a piece of common land next to St. John's Church, which was used by us children as a playground throughout most of the year, but was taken over in June to be the venue for the annual village fete and for the funfair when it rolled into town.

Roundabouts, a coconut-shy where you could win a goldfish, a helter-skelter and candy floss booth were set up. Music then blared out, tempting the faithful to come and enjoy themselves.

A big marquee was erected and the village rallied round to take part in the competitions to find the biggest marrow, the best home-made jam or the most creative flower arrangement. Mrs Garton was the chairwoman of the organising committee.

The gauntlet had been thrown down last year, when

both organisations had banned Aunt Lillian from attending their meetings. Now my aunt clearly felt she had an opportunity to get her own back.

"What has 'the dog having fleas' got to do with anything?" I asked a little tentatively, pushing the model to the centre of the table. I could feel another plan being hatched and that usually meant trouble in our family.

"I've been thinking and have come up with this marvellous plan," squealed my aunt with glee. "We will create our very own Fred Karno's circus, and the villagers will flock in from far and wide. We'll be able to charge them all sixpence to enter.

"I can see it now. We will make lots of money and that will be one in the eye of those hoity-toity women who thought to get the better of me."

I laughed to myself. Anyone thinking to get the better of Aunt Lillian usually came away with egg on their face, and, being a mischievous child, I was game for anything. It was only later on in life that I learnt to walk away at the first inkling of a plan by my aunt to out-wit someone in the village. At that time it usually meant fun and games.

"How will the dog having fleas make a circus possible? I queried.

"You have no imagination. We will set up a flea circus, of course!" Aunt Lillian chuckled. "We just have to catch some of the fleas, and it will be your job to train them to do tricks. They can jump through hoops, walk the tightrope and look; I have already made a little see-saw for them."

I shuddered at the thought. Why had I asked the question? I should have learned by now that usually the worst jobs fell to me.

She picked up the list again and cried out: "We can have snail racing, and we will make a race track with six lanes on which the snails can compete. There will be a prize for those picking the winner."

She was now getting into her stride and ideas were coming thick and fast. Feeling myself getting caught up in the rush of her enthusiasm, I suggested: "Perhaps slugs would be better, because they don't have to carry their houses on their backs and they would have a better turn of speed."

"That's a good idea," she retorted. "Get Neville and your other friends to come over and they can set about collecting those pesky slugs and snails that are eating my lettuces. This would be a much better use for them. At least they would earn their keep. The boys can also draw some big signs, and we will get your cousin Trevor to come over and set them up."

"How about an obstacle course?" I asked, excitedly. I could see Aunt Lillian's eyes sparkling behind her glasses with enthusiasm for the idea.

"Pegotty could drive the ducks round it, and people could pay to guess the time it takes," she declared. "We could use your uncle's stopwatch, and offer a prize for the person who guesses the correct time."

"I would put down five hours," I said dismissively at

the thought of giving such a task to her dog. "You know Pegotty isn't a very bright dog, and I am not sure she would be able to drive the ducks in a straight line, let alone around an obstacle course. The ducks are not much brighter – they would probably just fly off. Are you sure that's a good idea?"

"We could clip their wings to stop them flying away," said my aunt, undeterred. "That is what they do to the ravens at the Tower of London. Do you know there is a myth that if the ravens leave the Tower, then England will fall? Perhaps they forgot to clip them and that is why we had the war."

Warming to her 'master plan' theme, she added: "You could ask Nurse Johnson to lend us one of her new piglets. We could cover it with grease and the young men of the village could try to catch it. That would give everyone a laugh."

Not wanting to miss out on the fun, I made another suggestion. "How about a stall with the game called 'Blow the Woodlice into the Hole'?"

Aunt Lillian stopped in her tracks and scratched her head: "Never heard of that one. What do you do?"

"Well, we make a board with three tunnels in it, like a crazy golf course, only smaller," I explained. "You then get a straw, and when the woodlouse has rolled up into a ball, you blow it through the three tunnels and drop it into a hole. If you can do that you win a prize."

"I like that idea," enthused my aunt. "I am pleased to

see that you really do have some imagination. I was beginning to despair of you and thought you were going to be one of those dull children who seem to be rife in this village." She gave me a big grin and patted me, none too gently, on the head, causing my hair to become even more ruffled than it had been previously.

But her congratulations didn't last long. "Don't just stand there child. Go and rally the troops. We have lots to do, and, remember, the boys will have to find a supply of woodlice as well. We will keep them all in the shed until the big day."

"Won't Uncle Arthur object if we put the slugs and snails in there?" I asked. "He is always trying to get rid of them. You know how he puts beer traps down to catch them. He said it gives them a humane death." I laughed at the thought of drunken snails staggering around the garden. I had certainly seen those wiggly silver trails on the path.

"Are you aware the French eat snails?" mused by aunt. "Perhaps we could cook some and serve them in bridge rolls, with mustard and cress and Heinz salad cream. It could catch on as the snack of the month.

"We will have to provide some catering for our guests. All the best events have catering and I could make my special cakes."

"Oh no, please Auntie. Anything but your special cakes! They were really disgusting the last time you made them," I shuddered at the memory. Marmite covered sponge cakes were not one of my favourites. My aunt had a knack of creating specialities that were completely inedible.

"It wasn't my fault. I thought I was using chocolate spread," she insisted.

Sandwiches made from tinned dog food had once made their way onto the tea table, and she had been known to ice some dog biscuits when the little iced gems had run out.

Aunt Lillian suddenly announced that she would dress up as Gypsy Rose Lee. She informed me: "I will tell fortunes – good ones if they cross my palm with silver and bad ones if they try it with a threepenny bit or anything less than a sixpence. If Mrs Garton comes I will put a curse on her and make warts grow on her nose."

"I don't think Mrs Garton will visit," I said, chuckling at the thought of the rather stately lady finding that a big wart had suddenly grown on the end of her nose.

My thoughts were interrupted by my aunt coming up with a new idea. "Another attraction could be 'Milk the Goat'. If we put the goat behind a screen, people would have to put their arms through and pull on the udders to direct a stream of milk into a pail. Anyone who gets milk in the pail can take it home in a jug." She paused for a moment and started to laugh. "We could change the nanny for a billy goat sometimes – think of the confusion that would cause. It would be a grand wheeze."

"Can we have 'Splat the Rat' as well?" I asked. "That's

one of my favourites." I remembered how I had won a goldfish at the last summer fete.

"Well, what are you sitting there for Jojo?" my aunt demanded. "There's a lot to do and we have only a week to get everything done. Go and get your friends."

I left her sitting on the garden seat, dreaming of getting her own back on Mrs Garton, as I ran off to find my friends. They'd love it when I gave them the latest news of the alternative village fete that my aunt was planning.

Needless to say, it did not go as she intended!

# CHAPTER 7

# There's Now't So Queer as Folk

"I have just seen Smokey Joe! He is back in the woods again. Where do you think he has been these last few weeks?" I shouted as I came into Aunt Lillian's garden.

"Oh, he's back, is he? He's as mad as a hatter you know. He has probably been in the Queen's hotel, residing there at her pleasure," replied my aunt, laughing to herself, "but I've told you before not to go near him."

"I don't think the Queen would entertain him at Buckingham Palace," I said. "He's filthy, his clothes are all torn and he smells horrid. Anyway, I didn't go near him, I just saw the smoke from his fire when I came past. Do you think he is cooking hedgehogs again or perhaps he's caught a squirrel this time?" I flung myself down on the grass, next to my aunt, who was just putting the finishing touches to her newest creation. A shell sculpture was emerging in the flower bed and I had come over to help. She told me it was going to be a sundial, but I had my doubts about that.

Smokey Joe was the local tramp who lived in a bivouac in the woods near Aunt Lillian. His home was made from branches that he cut down and thatched with leaves and tarpaulins. It was like a wigwam and he would light a fire over which he would boil his billycan.

He was often seen in the village, wheeling a bicycle that had no tyres. All his worldly belongings were piled on top of it, like on one of the camels who plied the Spice Route from exotic lands.

We children would often follow, shouting after him. He would suddenly turn around, shake his grimy fist at us and shout "Get out of here!" causing us to scream and run off. We would sometimes dare each other to try to take something out of one of the bundles piled on the saddle. If we succeeded he would bare his teeth and shout: "Thieves and vagabonds — that's what you children are. You'll never get to heaven as the Good Lord will reject you and throw you down into the jaws of the devil. Just see if he doesn't."

My aunt had told me that he would catch hedgehogs and squirrels, cover them in mud and then bake them on his fire. When he peeled away the clay, the prickles would come off and the meat tasted just like chicken. I never did find out how she knew this.

Smokey Joe was by no means the only oddity. Most of Aunt Lillian's neighbours were eccentrics, as she was herself; perhaps there was something in the water or maybe they just naturally migrated to the end of the village that petered off into the woods.

In today's world the social services would have been poking their noses in and checking up on them, but then life worked at a slower pace and neighbours' differences were often celebrated. Perhaps that is the reason why my aunt fitted so well into the community.

While we were talking, there was some loud banging, and I asked what it was.

"It's just him next door," my aunt said scornfully. "Banging and crashing at all times of the day and night. He has no consideration for others. Says he is building a house and needs to drive nails in when necessary."

This was another of my aunt's unconventional neighbours. Old Man Brinkworth, as he was known in the village, was building his own house on the plot of land adjacent to Alva Lodge.

My aunt's house had been called Alva Lodge to honour her family's names – Arthur, my uncle, Lillian and Vera and Avis, their two daughters. She said it added gravitas to the family, like a coat of arms, and my uncle went along with the plan, being grateful that she had not decided on a more outlandish name for the property.

It was reputed that Mr. Brinkworth had been cashiered from the Indian Army for what was known as 'fraternising with the natives'. He had acquired the habit of working on the house dressed only in a loin cloth or dhoti which was favoured by the people of that country.

He was a thin, bald man who wore small wire glasses,

perched on the end of his nose, and leather 'Jesus' sandals. He was burnt to a nut brown colour by the suns of the distant empire, and people said he looked somewhat like Gandhi as he clambered over the home-made scaffolding he had erected around the house. Building regulations were more lax in those days. Homes were required to replace those lost in the war and permission was often given on the nod, that's if anyone applied for it in the first place.

On the other side of the lane lived Nurse Johnson, a very strange plump woman, who kept pigs in her back garden. Other people had chickens or rabbits, but Aunt Lillian's neighbour was different – she kept six large white saddlebacks in three pigsties downwind from her house but upwind of Aunt Lillian's.

Suddenly a gust of wind blew over the garden and the air was filled with a noisome smell of rotten food and pig manure.

"Go tell that woman to turn down the gas and shut the door of her shed," instructed my aunt. "When she starts cooking the smell is overpowering, and I am fed up with telling her that the brew she is stewing up will kill those animals before too long. Good riddance I say if they do go, but I am sure she will only get replacements. Why are some people so difficult and inconsiderate?"

Aunt Lillian was holding her nose as she got up from her knees. "I won't be able to work out here anymore until after feeding time." She stomped off towards the kitchen door.

I jumped up quickly. "Sorry, Aunty, I must go. I promised Nurse Johnson that I would stir the pigs' swill, and I don't want to be late."

To cut down on the cost of feeding the pigs, Nurse Johnson had come up with an admirable solution to deal with any village leftovers. In the days before re-cycling had grabbed the headlines, war time austerity was still affecting the national psyche and vegetable trimmings, apple cores and any leftovers were scraped into the dustbins that she had put around the village. These bins were chained to lamp posts and were marked 'Pig food' in large white letters, but as to why she thought anyone would want to take the bins remained a mystery. They stank to high heaven.

I was pulling on my wellingtons, when I remembered something. "I think she is going to kill Old Sally tomorrow," I announced, "can I go over and watch? I have never seen a pig killed before."

When Nurse Johnson slaughtered one of her animals she used to sell the meat off the back of her lorry – and very good meat it was too and everyone in the village rejoiced in the surfeit of pork. Meat rationing had only just finished and a Sunday roast was now back on the menu for special occasions for those who could afford it.

"No, you can't go and watch," said Aunt Lillian firmly. "You are only a child, you know. What do you want with going over there to watch such a gruesome event? Bloodthirsty, that's what you are. Isn't it bad enough that you go over and stir up that witches' brew that she cooks each afternoon?

"Anyway, it's not Christmas for a few months and she never kills her pigs until then."

As necessity is the mother of invention, Nurse Johnson had rigged up a 'Heath Robinson' contraption in her lean-to which consisted of a chipped enamel bath that had ball and claw feet, with two long gas jets under it. These were lit and the food remains were boiled up into a stew fit for her ladies, as she put it. I loved to go over there and stir the evil smelling concoction with a long paddle to make sure that it did not stick to the sides and burn.

Health and safety rules and regulations did not apply in those days.

"I am off now," I called as I rushed to the gate.

"Don't be late for tea and don't forget to change out of your clothes in the conservatory, I will leave some clean ones out for you. I don't want you bringing that stink back into my kitchen," Aunt Lillian called after me, "and, if she does kill the pig, try to put in a good word for me with regard to a leg of pork whilst you are at it!"

Yes, my dear aunt could sometimes be hypocritical.

Each year a set of temporary neighbours arrived at the beginning of summer, when the gypsies camped in a clearing in the woods. The men were there for the fruit picking and any other odd jobs they could scrounge. They tethered their horses in the lane and parked their brightly coloured traditional caravans in a circle, like a wagon train drawn up in formation, as if to protect them from an unlikely attack by the villagers. They were pure Romany and the women spent their time making pegs and wax flowers that they sold door to door.

As autumn approached the children collected heather from the heath and the women bound it up into small bunches which they sold near the Post Office. They would call out: "Lucky heather, lady. Buy some lucky heather. It will bring you riches beyond compare and fat healthy children."

If you did not buy from them, they muttered curses under their breath and tried to put the evil eye on reluctant purchasers.

As a child I loved to creep up and watch them from a safe distance, hidden behind a tree. They were so exotic and their colourful caravans were a magnet to many of the village children. Each afternoon, after the gypsies arrived back, one of the men would take out a fiddle and play merry jigs, while their children would dance and sing to the music. We so wanted to join them but had been warned that the gypsies often stole village children and took them away, never to be seen again.

For myself, I thought this might have some advantages, as gypsy children did not go to school and seemed to be having so much fun all the time.

Believe it or not, there was a nudist colony in the woods near Aunt Lillian's house and we had strict instructions not to go near it. Of course, we ignored these rules and often crept up to the sacking fence that surrounded the area, trying to peep at the naked people. The sacking was strung from wires to keep out prying eyes, but village children would use penknives and cut slits to peer through.

The novelty soon wore off as I never managed to see anyone at all, let alone anyone in their birthday suit.

All these characters were part of life at the end of the village that bordered onto the woods and I often thought of poor Mr and Mrs Wilcox who had the bungalow that backed on to Aunt Lillian's. They were a normal elderly couple who just wanted a quiet life and must have been puzzled by this strange community that surrounded them.

With such unconventional neighbours Aunt Lillian did not seem so out of place. She fitted well into this little community of strange characters.

## CHAPTER 8

# We're All Going to the Zoo Tomorrow

Big cats have always been a favourite of mine and a trip to the zoo was my idea of heaven. Aunt Lillian would allow us to choose a trip for our birthdays and every time I opted for Regent's Park Zoo. My brother Mikey, like me, always chose the same treat – but his was very different to mine. He loved trains, and wanted to go to a main line station, sit at the end of the platform and take down train numbers, which was not much to the liking of my aunt.

This was in the era before concerns about paedophiles and little boys sitting alone unsupervised on station platforms. Boys in those days collected books of train numbers which they avidly crossed off, trying to get a whole set of a particular class. My parents and aunt felt this was rather odd and totally pointless, but it was also harmless and it kept my brother out of mischief.

Being fair, Lillian did go with him on one occasion and tried to help, but when he returned home he emphatically told my mother that he would rather die than take her with him again. She was a total embarrassment; a view held by my mother in particular.

In retrospect, I think my mother particularly felt the burden of having such an eccentric relative.

As I said, my choice was London Zoo, and this particular day we set off with our packed lunch as we headed for the capital.

Sitting on the top of the 96 trolley-bus with Aunt Lillian, I exclaimed excitedly: "Let's sing our special song." So we both sang out loudly:

"We're all going to the zoo tomorrow,

*Zoo tomorrow, zoo tomorrow;*

Auntie's taking me to the zoo tomorrow,

We can stay all day."

Followed by the chorus…

"We're going to the zoo, zoo, zoo.

How about you? You can come, too.

We're going to the zoo, zoo, zoo.

You can stay all day."

… and numerous other verses about monkeys, elephants and kangaroos.

After a while a shout came from downstairs: "Quiet up top, please! You're disturbing the peace."

My aunt and I broke into fits of giggles, because this always happened when we struck up our song of the day. This was one of the rare situations when my aunt accepted defeat and we then sat quietly looking out of the window.

On every trip I would prematurely inquire if we were

nearly there, to which my aunt would give the same response.

"Jojo, you know we can't possibly be there yet. We have only just started, so why do you keep asking?"

I don't think Aunt Lillian realised that I was only asking because I knew it would get her going – or perhaps she did and just went along with it. This became our little joke, and I would regularly repeat the question throughout the journey. I'd eventually get the response I wanted: "Let's play 'I-spy' or 'The Minister's Cat', then we will not notice how long it takes to get there."

My favourite game of the moment was 'The Minister's Cat' which entailed one person stating that "The minister's cat is an atrocious cat" and the other person replying "The minister's cat is an acrobatic cat." This continued, through the alphabet, using a different word each time to describe the cat. The object was to find the longest and the most unusual words that could be applied to the cat. We had often played this and were experts at finding new and funny words that made us both giggle.

"When we get there, can we have our lunch watching the lions and tigers, please?" I cajoled. My request stemmed from the fact that my aunt had shown me a wonderful book in which there was a picture of an androgynous child in a white frock, walking in the Garden of Eden, with a hand on the head of a lion and a tiger. I almost wanted to die, so that I could go to this marvellous place and walk with the animals.

"Where else would we have lunch?" my aunt responded. "That is where we always go, and today will be no exception."

The journey could be tortuous for us, as we both had a fear of escalators, which were in many of the underground stations. I was sure that I would get caught in the teeth at the bottom and go down into the bowels of the earth and never see the light of day again. This caused us to find an alternative bus route, or to use tube stations that did not have escalators or lifts. Being a slightly nervous child at the time, I did not like lifts either, so sometimes it meant a long arduous climb up the emergency stairs as the only way to get out.

We always entered the zoo by the same gate, and this had a tall revolving iron contraption which, I again thought I might get trapped in. I was very relieved when I got out the other side. I must have been a wimpy kid, but my aunt was always willing to indulge fantasies and beliefs that were different, because she often felt the same way.

First stop was the seals, as I loved to watch them diving into the water and enjoyed the whole process of seeing them swim. As a child, I hated water and just wished I could feel that free. The seals looked as though they were having tremendous fun and encouraging each other to perform antics for an appreciative audience. Their soft black eyes would look at you for approval, as if to say "what did you think of that then?"

"I wish we could feed them with fish," I said wistfully.

Aunt Lillian told me: "You would get really smelly, but we can come back later and watch the man feeding them. Let's see what time that happens and we can return then. Well, where to next?"

At that point a strong gust of wind blew, and Aunt Lillian's perky little red hat flew into the water. A seal swam over, pushed his nose into it and carried it away. He swam round and round several times.

"Oh, no!" squealed my aunt. "That was one of my favourites. Bring it back this instance, you naughty animal." She could not help but smile when the seal came over to us and offered the hat back to her. It was as though it had understood her.

Taking the wet hat from the seal, she wrung it out and plonked it back on her head. "Thank you so much, Mr. Seal." She gave a little curtsey and turned to me.

"Do you want to see the penguins now?" she asked. I did, so we wandered over to their enclosure.

I loved the way they waddled over a bridge in a huddle, like little old men in dinner suits. I was also captivated by how they changed when they entered the water, from clumsy clowns to under water torpedoes, streaking around the small pool. Again they seemed to be doing it just for fun.

We watched them for some time, laughing at their antics, but I knew what my aunt wanted to see. Her favorite was Guy the gorilla. Looking at him, she told me:

"Did you know he arrived at the zoo clutching a tin hot water bottle on Guy Fawkes Day in 1947? It was really cold that November day and he would not let go of it. Look at him; he is such a gentle creature for something so big and wild."

Guy always seemed puzzled by the attention he received from the crowd who gathered around and sometimes poked fun at him. Aunt Lillian was angry at this discourtesy to a noble creature, as she called him, and had been known to remonstrate with a child for such rudeness. In those days parents did not fly off to court to seek compensation if a total stranger told their child off.

Another stopping place was the Mappin Terraces to see the most famous polar bear of all time – Brumas. On November 27th, 1949, Brumas had been born at the zoo and named after her keepers, Bruce and Sam. The Press gave a lot of publicity to the first baby polar bear to be successfully reared in Britain, but incorrectly reported that the bear was a 'he' and the error was not corrected, so the public always thought Brumas was male.

Even in those days the Press got it wrong – sometimes!

Lunch time came and that meant the Lion House, which at that time was a cramped building with a concrete tiered viewing platform in front of very small cages housing lions, tigers, leopards and cheetahs. Here we could sit down and have our picnic.

I remember going there when I was very small and causing much hilarity because I asked in a loud voice which was the lion that made the ice cream. In those days Lyons Ice Cream was my favourite kind, and I could not understand why everyone laughed at my remark. Apparently, I was most put out.

As she sat down, Lillian removed her hat, and I started to giggle as her silver hair was now dyed a fetching shade of pink.

"Which lion do you think ate Albert?" she said. It was all part of our game.

"Albert who?" I asked in a loud voice, even though I knew the answer. I just loved the story that I knew would follow.

"Albert Ramsbottom, of course," she replied. "He was the naughty boy who went to the zoo and stuck a stick in the lion's ear. He got just what he deserved." She then began the famous Stanley Holloway tale of Albert and the Lion:

"There's a famous seaside town called Blackpool,
That's noted for fresh air and fun,
And Mr and Mrs Ramsbottom
Went there with young Albert, their son.
"A grand little lad was young Albert,
All dressed in his best; quite a swell
With a stick with an 'orse's 'ead 'andle
The finest that Woolworth's could sell."

The story went on forever, and I wriggled with delight when she reached the part where the lion, called Wallace, ate up young Albert. By then a crowd had gathered around to listen. My aunt was quite a performer, and I know she considered sending her hat round to collect coins from her audience.

When she was finished and the crowd had dispersed, we laid out our picnic on the large red spotted handkerchief that my aunt kept especially for this purpose.

Suddenly we noticed a rather fat woman poking fun at one of the lions. We both hated to see that, so were most amused when the lion suddenly rose, stretched itself with a big yawn, cocked his leg up and peed all over the woman.

We collapsed into fits of giggles as she ran out shouting: "Where is the keeper? I am going to have that lion shot."

Unfortunately, we had to pack up and leave, because a strong smell of lion pee overwhelmed us, but we both felt the lion had given the woman what she deserved.

After continuing our lunch outside under the trees, we consulted the map and decided to visit the monkey house. In retrospect this would have been construed as a mistake, but I was young and foolish then and loved my aunt dearly so I was not too put out by her antics which included jumping up and down making monkey faces while tucking her hands in her armpits.

I asked her with the seriousness that only comes from a child: "Why is it OK to make fun of the monkeys when you were so annoyed with the people poking fun at Guy the gorilla?"

"Monkeys love it," countered Aunt Lillian. "Just look at them. They are such happy go lucky creatures, whereas Guy is a thoughtful giant who has the look of a philosopher and should be respected as such."

"Come on, Jojo, why don't you join in and make them laugh for a change? For a child, you really are a bit of a stick in the mud, you know."

We saw the giraffes, the parrots and the kangaroos as well as the elephants and rhinoceros, which reminded us of ancient creatures that had descended from the dinosaurs. We finished up exhausted, but had enjoyed a fantastic day.

Upon arriving home, I had tea and then went early to bed to dream of the animals I had seen. I would promise myself that I would ask for the same treat again next year.

Those days live on in my memory, as Aunt Lillian was always able to see things from a child's point of view and join in on their level. This was what made her such a great companion and why so many children regularly came to visit her.

# CHAPTER 9

# To Die Will be an Awfully Big Adventure

"Are you looking forward to dying, Jojo?" Aunt Lillian asked as I entered her house through the back door on a bright and breezy Saturday morning.

"Can't say I've thought about it much," I answered quickly. It seemed a strange question to ask, as death was a far away improbability from my childish perspective. "Why are you asking anyway?"

"Aristotle and Peter Pan thought that to die would be an awfully big adventure, and I think it will be as well. I have been studying the subject and preparing for the inevitable. I would like it to be a big adventure."

"Well, you are old, so I suppose you are going to die soon," I said thoughtlessly as I walked over to the kitchen table and sat down.

"Not so much of the old, my girl," she snapped. "I will have you know that you are only as old as you feel, and I feel young at the moment. Perhaps not in years, but in my mind I am only a bit older than you."

"I suppose you're right," I agreed. "Mum often says that you must be in your second childhood. Do all adults get a second crack at it? I was looking forward to growing up, but if I have to do it all again, I am not so sure. I enjoy school most of the time, but I wouldn't like to have to learn to read or learn my times tables again. Will you have to go back to school?"

"I knew your mother said horrid things about me behind my back," said my aunt waspishly, wrinkling her nose to show her disapproval. "She has a wicked tongue on her, but don't you go telling her that." She winked at me. "To answer your question, no, Jojo, I will not have to go back to school."

"I have been reading this book and, apparently, when you die the angels come down and carry you up to Heaven. They dress you in flowing robes of white, blue, silver or gold."

This revelation intrigued me. I loved dressing up and the robes sounded fantastic. I could see myself sweeping up the steps of Heaven, clothed from head to toe in cloth of gold. I would certainly make an entrance and everyone would look at me. It would be like a red carpet event, and God would be sitting there on his throne welcoming me.

"Why do you have different colour dresses?" I wanted to know.

"They are not dresses, they are robes, and it very much depends on the state of grace that you are in when you expire."

"What does expire mean?" I asked.

"Die, it means to die, and you get a robe that signifies how good you have been during your lifetime. Gold is the very pinnacle of goodness, followed by silver, then blue and white."

Heaven obviously has a class system, I thought. "What happens then?" I asked excitedly. Death seemed to have a lot going for it and I had been pretty good over the past week, so I might be in with a chance of qualifying for a gold robe. Gold was my favourite colour, after all.

"Well, after the angels have deposited you in Heaven, you wander in a soft mist, listening to the strains of the angelic hosts," Aunt Lillian explained. "I suppose this is a kind of divine Muzak, and I hope it has an off button because I find background music very irritating. You have to spend that time contemplating your sins."

"When you fully repent and seek forgiveness, the mists will be parted and you'll be led into a beautiful garden. All your heart's desires will be given to you and you'll live there for all eternity."

"Is this option available to everyone? Will the Vicar's wife get in?" I asked mischievously. "You said she was a sinful woman, so will there be a place for her? If there is, I hope that she gets a blue or white frock." I knew my aunt had fallen out with the Vicar's wife again and they were not on speaking terms.

"I keep telling you it is not a frock or a dress, it is a robe," Aunt Lillian corrected. "A robe is something quite different, and that is what they wear up there," she said, pointing to the sky. "The Vicar's wife will probably get in. Although she is two-faced and a dreadful gossip, she is not wicked, so I suspect she will qualify, but she might have to wear a grey robe until she sees the error of her ways."

Lillian always saw things from her own point of view and was quick to focus on other people's sins whilst being blind to her own.

"What will happen to really wicked people, like Hitler or Vlad the Impaler?" I asked.

She thought about this for a moment before coming up with an answer. "I am not sure, but I know the Bible says that God forgives all sinners if they repent. So I suppose they will have to be given the opportunity to wander in the mists, too, but I'm sure they will not reach the state of grace that is required for promotion to the next level. They will be pushed back into the mists and are probably still walking around there to this day."

"I hope I don't bump into them in the fog," I whispered. "They scare me – perhaps dying is not such a big adventure. It could be dangerous."

"You're right, Jojo. If they are still wandering aimlessly in the foggy depths of purgatory, we might bump into them on our exit from this world. Or perhaps they will be in a different part of the mist and have to carry bells like the lepers did in the olden days. That way we will be able to hear them coming and take avoiding action. I am sure God in his wisdom has that kind of thing sorted out."

I always admired my aunt's practical mind. She had an answer for everything. Now her eyes were sparkling behind her spectacles and she leaned forward in her chair as she warmed to her theme.

"That garden is the original Garden of Eden which has been vacant since the fall of Adam and Eve. You must have heard of Adam and Eve at Sunday School."

I nodded my head. Somehow Lillian felt that the world began and ended within her limited concept of time.

"Eve was a wicked hussy, you know – she led poor Adam astray by giving him an apple when she was told not to touch them."

"Why is touching an apple so bad?" I asked. "You always say, an apple a day keeps the doctor away, so why did Eve get in so much trouble?"

"God told her not to touch the apples from the Tree of Life, but she just ignored him and you do that at your peril. Then the Devil sneaked out from behind the tree, disguised as a serpent, and tempted her, so she picked an apple and gave it to poor Adam and took one for herself. When they both gobbled them up they were thrown out of the Garden of Eden and that's why it has been vacant ever since. "I am pleased to see that it is now being put to good use as the new age Shangri-la for the 20th century. There you will have all that your heart desires and more. You only have to think of what you want and it will appear."

I gave this some thought. I would certainly have to be

more careful about scrumping apples this year. There might be consequences, so I would have to remember to look out for passing snakes in Mr. Brinkworth's garden. I'd seen a snake there last summer and had obviously had a close shave.

Aunt Lillian continued dreamily: "I will not have any meals to make because you just think of your favourite dinner and there it will be on golden platters, spread out for the taking. When you have finished it will just disappear, so that will take care of the washing up."

She always had delusions of grandeur since she had read about the Queen having a solid gold dinner service.

"Heaven seems really fantastic," I enthused. "They haven't told me about that part yet at Sunday School. I will ask Miss Clements what she knows about Heaven next week."

"There is more to look forward to, Jojo," my aunt assured me. "When I think of my dog, Pegotty, she will magically materialise and I will take her for long walks through the woods. I will never get tired and she will keep running after sticks and splashing in the river, but when she shakes herself, I will not get wet or muddy. Just think of that." She smiled to herself. "When the walk is over she will just vanish. No vet's bills to worry about, no barking and annoying the neighbours, no pooper scoops – Pegotty will be the perfect pet."

"Are you sure Pegotty will be there in Heaven?" I

challenged her. "The Vicar told us that animals do not have souls and so when they die, that's that."

"What does the Vicar know about Heaven?" she retorted. "He is just a Vicar."

"Isn't that what Vicars do?" I persisted. "I thought they had a special relationship with God."

"No, that is just what they tell children to make them listen," came the reply from a woman who was doing exactly the same sort of thing herself – but on a far bigger scale! "God is not stupid, you know. He made Pegotty, so he will want Pegotty to go back to him and play in the Garden of Eden. It will be a dull and dreary place if there are no animals there and what are we going to eat if there are no lambs, cows or pigs? I don't fancy becoming a vegetarian at this stage in my life."

"What else is there to look forward to?" I was getting quite excited about it.

"Gramophones and the radio won't be necessary, as you will just think of the music you want and it will waft through the air at the exact volume required. Rock or pop, classical or opera – it will all be there for our enjoyment." She hummed a little tune to herself at the thought.

"Friends can be conjured up in the twinkling of an eye, and, when you get fed up with them, they will be consigned back to the big filing cabinet in the sky until the next time."

I liked the sound of this as I found it a drag going over

to see my best friend who lived on the other side of the village. I would be able to magically call her up and she would be there in an instant.

"If everybody gets a chance to get in, won't Heaven be really crowded?" I asked.

"Don't be ridiculous!" my aunt scoffed. "God has thought of that and we will all be allocated our own small worlds, quite separate from one another, except when we want to communicate, and then we conjure people up, as I have just told you. It has been scientifically proven that space is infinite and the universe has no boundaries."

"All this space will definitely be needed. There are millions and millions of people in the world, and countless thousands have died in the past," I said.

Lillian got to her feet and picked up the cups and saucers. "All this thinking about death has made me hungry," she said. "Put the kettle on and I will get out some Garibaldi biscuits I bought yesterday."

"Can't we have Jaffa Cakes instead? I don't like Garibaldi's – they look like they have dead flies in them." I shuddered at the thought.

"They are not flies, but they could be mouse droppings you know," she teased me, laughing out loud. "Just think, we would not have to get up from our chairs if we were in Heaven now – we could just think about a nice cup of tea and a plate of biscuits and, 'abracadabra', there they would be."

I can only hope that my aunt found death to be a big

adventure and I am disappointed that she has not seen fit to send back messages to me to tell me that her beliefs were true. If they are, then I, too, will be looking forward to death with a new sense of optimism. Her view of Heaven was quite magical, and premature suicide could have been on the cards after spending time listening to her interpretation of life after death.

Aunt Lillian lived her life as an elderly Peter Pan who never wanted to grow up; she felt that happiness was the meaning of life, the whole aim and end of human existence. Her version of happiness often caused problems for others, but she was usually unaware of this, and my childhood was spent sharing her many adventures.

# CHAPTER 10

# I Can Do That Blindfolded!

"Oh, bligger, blugger!" I shouted, looking around to make sure I had not been overheard, as my mum always gave me a clip round the ear for just thinking bad words, even if I didn't say them.

I put my hand up to my nose to see if it was bleeding, as I had bumped it on the back door after tripping on the step in my impatience to call round to see the new kitten. Fortunately it wasn't.

Why was the door locked? This was strange as my aunt always left the doors open. Had she fallen or been taken ill? I knocked loudly several times. She was never out at this time of the day, so there must be a problem.

Then I heard footsteps. "All right, all right! What is the hurry? Is there a fire or something? I am coming, give me a chance."

I heard a few bangs and crashes and then the door was flung open. Lo and behold, there was my Aunt Lillian with a blindfold on. A bright red spotted handkerchief was tied round her eyes and the corner hung down over her nose.

I could not hide my surprise. I was so used to seeing

her staring at me with her small grey eyes through her National Health Glasses. "Why are you wearing a handkerchief over your eyes – are you playing Blind Man's Bluff or something? Can I join in? Is there a party?"

She reached out towards me and answered: "Come on in quickly and stop asking stupid questions. No, there is not a party and I am not playing Blind Man's Bluff. Whatever gave you that silly idea?"

As strange happenings were not unusual when visiting Aunt Lillian, I obeyed and followed her slowly into the kitchen. On the way she almost crashed into the hall stand, knocking a walking stick over, and causing a couple of coats to fall to the floor. Before picking them up, I deftly caught the vase that tottered on the edge of the hall table and put it back in place. Then I noticed that the newspapers were still on the floor behind the door. At that moment my aunt cracked her shoulder on the door frame and let out a yelp.

"Well, what exactly are you doing?" I asked. "I just came round after school and found the back door locked. I was so surprised; I bumped my head trying to get in." I rubbed my nose again. "But you are in danger of doing yourself a greater injury with that blindfold on."

Not answering any of my questions, she held up her hand for silence. Then she said casually: "Would you like a cup of tea and some Jaffa Cakes? I got a new packet this morning, when I dropped into the Co-op."

"Yes, I would, but I still want to know what you are doing."

We moved into the kitchen where she went to the Aga cooker and picked up the kettle, banging into the table on the way. Having filled it, she tottered back to the stove, spilling water as she went, but managed to put it on the hotplate and make her way to the cupboard to get the cups and saucers. Disaster was looming as they were piled up, one on top of the other, and I could imagine them all tumbling down and breaking into lots of pieces.

I offered to help, but was sharply told: "Sit down and wait, will you. You are always asking so many questions. Questions, questions, questions. When you grow up, you will realise that you have to practise if you want to get better at things, so that is what I am doing – practising. It is obvious, isn't it?"

It was not obvious to me, but it was always easier to give in and do as I was told, so I drew out a couple of chairs and pulled them up to the table. In the centre was an open box of Jaffa Cakes with a plate beside it, but the cakes were laid out on the table cloth! I was puzzled.

We waited in silence for the kettle to boil and eventually it began to sing out. My aunt picked up the teapot, poured the water in and brought it to the table with no further mishaps.

"I am not going to say anything until we have finished our tea." She could be very annoying at times.

"Shall I lay out cups and saucers and pour the tea then?" I asked.

"No, we need to wait for it to brew. Anyway, what

brought you round here in such a rush?"

"I wanted to see the new kitten," I replied. "What have you decided to call it?"

At that moment a rather large black and white kitten climbed out of the basket by the side of the Aga, stretched and came towards me.

"I've called him Tiny Wee," she said with a straight face.

Why, he's hardly tiny? In fact, he is huge for a kitten," I said, putting out my hand towards him. Tiny Wee ignored it.

"I know he is quite big for his age, but he keeps doing tiny wees all over the place and so I thought it would be the perfect name for him."

We both started to giggle. My aunt had an answer for everything, but she didn't do herself any favours when she added: "He even weed on the back door step – that's probably why you tripped."

When we had calmed down, I noticed that she looked very smug. She asked: "Well, aren't you interested to know why I am doing all the chores blindfolded?"

"Of course I am, but you told me to wait for the answer until we had finished tea."

Picking up the teapot, she felt around for the cup and poured, but only hot water came out; she had forgotten to put the tea leaves into the pot.

I decided to play her at her own game and, stifling my giggles, I let her carry on.

Aunt Lillian passed me the cup of hot water and felt around for the plate on which she assumed she had placed the Jaffa Cakes. On finding it, she proceeded to pass an empty plate around.

By this time I couldn't contain myself any longer and burst out laughing. She was most indignant, demanding: "What is so funny?"

"You are funny," I exploded. "You should see yourself and what you have done. There's no tea in the pot and the cakes are not on the plate. Why on earth are you doing everything blindfolded?"

"Okay, I suppose explanations are now due," she sighed. "Do you know how many people lose their sight when they get older? Well, I have been thinking about it and I realised how difficult life would be so I have been practising doing all the jobs around the house blindfolded. That way, if I lost my sight I would be able to stay in my own home and not be a burden to anyone. I certainly have no intention of letting your mother put me in a home. I know she would like to get her sticky paws on this property – whatever she might say to the contrary."

"Mum doesn't want to do any such thing," I remonstrated. "Anyway, you are not old and you won't go blind." I said this because it was the sort of thing you are supposed to say. She seemed pretty ancient to me, but perhaps that was because I was only eight.

"Well," she answered. "I want to retain my

independence as long as possible and so I am making every effort to do so. Practice makes perfect, you know."

This was one of her favourite homilies and one that she did not usually follow herself. It was always something she told other people to get them to do things for her.

"I can now make the bed, feed the cat and make a sandwich blindfolded. I am aiming to add a new task every week so that in time I will be able to do all the chores required to remain independent. What have you got to say to that?"

I just shook my head. What would she think of next?

"Has everything gone according to plan so far?" I asked sweetly.

"I have only had a couple of minor mishaps," she assured me. "Yesterday I made a sandwich with the tinned cat food. It tasted a bit like fishy corned beef, but it was quite nice actually, and I might just have it again. I know the cat was very pleased with the chicken I put down for him."

I looked down at the bowl on the floor and was shocked by what I saw in it. "Why has the cat got tinned plums for dinner?" I inquired. "I don't think he will like them, and even the dog, who normally scoffs anything, has left them alone."

"Oh, is that what they are?" Aunt Lillian said with a coy grin. "I didn't realise it was plums in the tin when I got it out of the larder – I thought it was Kitty-Kat."

"Sounds like you have eaten all the Kitty-Kat

yourself," I chuckled. How has the cleaning been going under your new system?"

Looking around the kitchen I thought that my aunt must have done it with the blindfold on. Cleaning was never her strong point, but on this occasion things looked more under par than normal. Dust balls were now forming at an alarming rate in the corners and the floor was covered with spots of food that the dog thought were too meagre to bother with.

"Do you keep the blindfold on all the time?" I asked.

"No, only for a couple of hours each day at the moment, but next week I intend to wear it when I go down the village to do the shopping."

I gasped in horror at the thought.

Undeterred, Aunt Lillian continued: "I have found one of your uncle's old walking sticks and I am going to paint it white. I have also been training Pegotty to be a guide dog."

Pegotty was a pretty crazy dog and I felt like telling my aunt that no sane person would want to put their life in her hands. Instead, I said: "That's asking an awful lot of Pegotty. Surely, it takes months to train a guide dog."

"She's not got the hang of it yet, but she just needs a little bit of practice," my aunt insisted. "I still have to get her harness right so that she can send me signals when we approach the kerbs and stop me walking in front of on-coming traffic."

I could hold back no more! "Auntie, she is over

fourteen and her sight is going, so I don't think she will be much help to you. It will be a matter of the blind leading the blind."

With that, Aunt Lillian pulled down the blindfold, looked at the tea things and said: "Well, if at first you don't succeed then try, try again."

I could not fault my aunt when it came to persistence and imagination, but her ideas were completely impracticable.

She was now in full cry: "I would have been a great Boy Scout — 'be prepared', that's my motto."

"Auntie," I said patiently, "Boy Scouts weren't taught to prepare by placing their lives in the hands of an elderly, eccentric, poorly-trained guide dog. You'll end up getting both of you killed. If you don't value your own life, surely you don't want to risk Pegotty's?"

Finally, she saw the point and never put her road crossing plan into action — at least, I hope she didn't!

## CHAPTER 11

# Hedging Her Bets

Our family were C of E, or at least that was what we put on forms when the question arose, but we were not attending church on a regular basis. In fact, we only went as a family when attendance, at events such as funerals, christenings and weddings, was obligatory. Easter and Christmas fell into the category of obligatory, as the hymns were great and we all liked singing lustily when the church was full. It didn't really matter then that most of us were off key and slightly behind the organ; when the volume was at full blast nobody noticed.

Aunt Lillian, however, was different; she decided in her late seventies that death was just around the corner and she may be going to meet her Maker sooner, rather than later (she actually lived well into her eighties). So she started a study of world religions to find out which offered the best 'after life', and this was the beginning of a difficult phase for all the family.

One Saturday I arrived early at her house. "Morning, Jojo," she called from the scullery, "I won't be a moment. Sit yourself down. I have just had a brainwave."

I could see problems on the horizon, because her so

called 'brainwaves' always spelled trouble, but sat down anyway.

At that moment, my aunt appeared draped in what looked like a large bright yellow sheet. Her arms were also bright yellow right up to her elbows. Under the sheet, her long sleeved vest showed and her tiny stockinged feet peeped out from the folds of cloth.

"What have you done to your arms?" I squealed. "They are all yellow – and why are you dressed like that?"

"Don't worry, I have done one for you as well, so you will not feel left out," she assured me. "We will be the start of a new band of brothers."

"If it is going to be us, won't it be a band of sisters?" I queried, somewhat puzzled.

Ignoring my remark, she continued: "I have come up with the right costumes and found a pair of clippers in the bathroom cabinet to help us look the part."

She promptly produced them and quickly proceeded to lay some newspapers on the floor. Then, grabbing a kitchen chair, she said: "Sit down here and undo your plaits. I'll just shave off those golden locks of yours – then you can do the same for me."

"What!" I screamed. "Why do you want to shave off my hair?" I was rather proud of it.

"Well, you can't join in with me if you are not willing to sacrifice something, and your hair seems a small price to pay to achieve paradise when you die," she replied, unconcerned about my feelings.

I had been talking about wanting to go to paradise after reading Aunt Lillian's book, but I did not realise that it entailed losing my hair. A child in one of the pictures in the book was walking with wild animals and had long golden curls. So how had she got into paradise without having her hair cut off, I asked myself? This was an image that had made a great impression on me and I thought that dying would be great fun, not walking about with yellow arms, draped in a sheet with a bald head. If that was the case, I was quite willing to give it a miss.

I was now getting really worried because my aunt was bearing down on me with a very determined look on her face. I protested strongly at this point: "Surely I don't need to lose all my hair. I think I will look really silly if I go to school with a bald head, and all the kids will make fun of me. Anyway, Mum will go loopy if I go home with no hair. You know she will."

Aunt Lillian retorted: "Your mother never commits herself to anything, but don't tell her I said that. She will go straight to hell and burn in eternal damnation if she doesn't start thinking about life after death and taking care of her eternal soul."

I didn't want my Mum to go to hell; I had seen pictures of the horrid things that the devil had in store for sinners. So I whispered: "You go first and then I might be able to pluck up the courage to let you cut my hair, if that is the only way to save Mum, and for me to go to Heaven."

Always one to take immediate action without thinking of the consequences, she sat on the seat and ran the clippers straight down the middle of her head, leaving a narrow furrow. This reminded me of the story of the Red Sea parting for the Israelites, which we had read about in Sunday School the previous week.

I gasped: "You look really funny now. I think you had better have a look in the mirror before you go any further."

With that I ran into her bedroom, grabbed the mirror from the dressing table and thrust it in front of her.

"Oh Lord! I do look a bit of a sight," she admitted. "I will not be able to go out without a hat for a month at least. Perhaps it will look better when it is all off." She started to laugh, shrugged her shoulders and went into the scullery to bring out another saffron coloured sheet and some bowls which she placed on the table.

My aunt was always very resilient in the face of insurmountable problems, and this disaster came into that category, as it was not possible to grow hair at will, so she was able to put it out of her mind and go on with her plan.

Spinning around to let me take a good look at her, she asked: "What do you think, does this colour suit me?"

I countered her question with one of my own: "You still haven't told me why you're dressed like that and why you want to shave our heads. What is going on?"

"Well, I thought we could become the first group of

Hare Krishna followers in our village," she finally explained. "I have been reading all about it in the local paper and have investigated what it entails. You walk around dressed in saffron robes, ringing bells and carrying begging bowls. I can save lots of money from the house keeping, because people have to put food in our begging bowls, so I will not have to cook lunch or anything. I think it is a very good wheeze, don't you?"

"No, I don't!" I exclaimed. "I really don't want to eat other people's leftovers. They might give us Brussels sprouts or cauliflower, which I hate."

"You are such a fussy eater," she said. "If you had lived through the war you would not be so difficult to feed. We were short of everything when Adolf was trying to rule the world and food was rationed, so you had to eat what you were given. It was one in the eye for him, if we ate all our home-grown vegetables."

"I don't like gravy or tapioca either," I mused. "If people scrapped that into our bowls it would be disgusting."

"You are right," she conceded. "I also dislike gravy and tapioca. We will have to think again about this religion. Perhaps it's not such a good idea after all."

With that, she let the sheet fall to the ground, and there she stood in her long pink drawers, wrinkly stockings and thick long sleeved vest. I had to giggle and told her: "Aunty, you look really funny, especially with that hairstyle."

This prompted her to say: "Jojo, put the kettle on while I get dressed, and we will go down to the library to find a religion that does not entail eating gravy or tapioca. I especially hate tapioca because it looks like snotty pudding."

Some minutes later she returned wearing her natty red hat and carrying a piece of paper. "I have been thinking about this for a long time," she revealed. "I am not getting any younger and the time has come when I ought to consider the 'hereafter' and the destination of my immortal soul. I need a plan of action, so I have written this list of the religions of the world and I can now cross off Hare Krishna. That is one down."

In the next few weeks she read books on various religions and tried to convert the rest of the family to each one. We needed to be saved and she felt that her mission was to take us all with her on her journey.

Needless to say, the family did not appreciate her quest for enlightenment or whatever she wanted to call it. It meant trouble for everyone, and we children were a prime target for her proselytizing, but we loved the stories she told us to illustrate the benefits of turning to one god or another.

Once she gathered us kids together in the kitchen to hear one of her sermons. She had placed two large baskets on the table and then informed us: "Today we are going to study 'The Feeding of the Five Thousand' – when Jesus took just five fishes and two loaves and fed a big crowd of people. I am not sure how he did it, but that is Jesus for you."

"I think you will find it was five loaves and two fishes, Mrs Auger," pointed out John. He was the Vicar's son, so I felt that he should know.

"Okay, whatever," Aunt Lillian accepted, waving him aside. "I just know that he fed lots of people, and we need to find out how he did it, as that would save money. He must have used some kind of magic trick."

"Have you got your magic wand, Mrs Auger?" Neville piped up. He was a little scared of my aunt, as he thought she was a kind of witch and might have magical powers. She had threatened to turn him into a frog once, and he had never forgotten it. He always gave the garden broom, which stood propped up by the door, a wide berth upon entering the kitchen. I am sure he thought she flew on it when the moon was full, and she had fuelled these stories on several occasions.

"No, Neville, I have not got a magic wand," she assured him. "I will just wave my hands over the baskets and they will fill up. I saw something similar on the David Nixon show last week. He is a magician, you know."

"I saw that programme and he made lots of rabbits appear," I chimed in.

"Well, rabbits would make a stew, so it can't be so different with fishes. Bring those baskets over here," she instructed.

We kids loved to take part and so rushed to help.

Aunt Lillian whisked the serviette off the top of the first basket and we peered inside. There at the bottom were five sardines on a plate. In the second basket there were two small bridge rolls.

"Now you see them," she announced, putting the cloths back over the top. "I will just say a spell and there will be enough to feed us all for lunch. We don't want enough food to feed five thousand, so I will make it a little spell for the first attempt."

"Izzy Wizzy, let's get busy," she intoned, waving her hands frantically over the two baskets.

"That's not a real spell because it's what Sooty says and it never works for him," I interrupted.

"Oh, ye of little faith, stop interrupting me when I am casting a spell, or it could go wrong and make all the food disappear," Aunt Lillian claimed. "Then I won't have anything for your uncle's tea. Anyway, Sooty is just a puppet, so it wouldn't work for him, but it will be different when I say it. You just wait and see. Now where was I?"

"Oh yes – Izzy Wizzy, let's get busy. Izzy Wizzy, make food appear!" With that, she whisked the serviette off the top and gazed into the basket. "Humph, it didn't work properly," she lamented. "I can't think why – perhaps I do need a wand after all, though Jesus didn't use one."

John decided it was time to put Lillian right by informing her: "Jesus was the Son of God and that is why he could perform miracles – that was how he fed the five thousand." Then he added, rather priggishly: "My dad says it is blasphemous to think that mere mortals can produce miracles."

"Well, your dad should know John, he is the Vicar, after all," replied my aunt. "I just thought it was worth a go, but I don't know what I would have done with lots of sardines. I don't really like them very much and Uncle Arthur would complain if he had to eat loads of them, so perhaps it is better that the spell didn't work." She smiled at us. "Let's have some home-made lemon barley water and make do with a packet of Jaffa Cakes."

Over the following months, Aunt Lillian also visited each of the churches in the village in turn, to sample different denominations. She had by this time given up on world religions and had come closer to home. She was certainly hedging her bets. Although it was a small village, there was a good choice, and God must have had us under his magnifying glass. St. Mary's down by the Mill, St. John's on Parkhill, the Congregational Church on Hurst Road and the Baptist Church in the High Street. The Methodists and Catholics also had a place in the heart of this small community. Upon reflection, we must have had many sinners as neighbours to need that level of pastoral care, but I am not sure that any god was ever going to be prepared for my aunt.

CHAPTER 12

# Welcoming God's Creatures

On Sunday mornings I was always packed off to church with Aunt Lillian so that my parents could have some peace and quiet. I think this was a big mistake on their part, as trouble usually ensued and I know they were ashamed, as they found my aunt's antics a particular source of embarrassment. I would have thought they would have preferred to keep an eye on her themselves. They often accused me of being her 'partner in crime' and I invariably got part of the blame if things went awry. So it should not have come as a surprise when this particular Sunday proved to be eventful.

As I arrived I saw Aunt Lillian coming out of the house, dressed up to the nines in her Sunday best, but she was leading her three ducks Pip, Squeak and Wilfred, who were wearing the little bow ties that she had made for them. She was holding a carrier bag full of windfalls and when I glanced at them I could see they were pretty maggoty.

She thrust the bag into my hand. "You can carry these.

They are our contribution to the Harvest Festival," she announced. "I have collected the best of the ones that were lying on the floor. I am not going to give my very best apples, as I am sure that the Vicar's wife 'steals' the pick of the produce and uses it herself."

My aunt and the Vicar's wife had been arch enemies for many years.

"That is not a very Christian thought," I pointed out. Then, looking at the ducks, I exclaimed: "Tell me that you are not thinking of taking them with us? I thought we were going to church."

"We are, and yes, I am taking them with us," came the firm reply. "After all, they are God's creatures and today happens to be Harvest Festival, so I think it would be very appropriate to take them into God's house."

"You are not going to give them to the church, are you?" I asked in amazement. "They might kill them and have them for dinner. They wouldn't have any use for live ducks. I think you are expected to take fruit or vegetables – not animals!"

Once again, in our close relationship it was a case of me, the child, trying to make my ageing aunt see sense.

"They are not my contribution," Aunt Lillian said, fixing a stern gaze on me through her glasses. "I just thought it would be nice if they could take part – Jesus always said suffer little animals to come unto me."

I explained that the Bible actually said 'Suffer little children' not animals, but this did not deter her.

"You are always so pedantic, Jojo," my aunt retorted stubbornly. "Well, I knew it was something like that, so I am taking them with me this week."

My heart sank. Taking the ducks out was a new fad of hers and they seemed to love the attention they received, but shopkeepers and bus conductors were appalled. I had been with her when she took them on the 132 bus and caused havoc, much to the amusement of the boys from the grammar school, who were among the passengers. The conductor had said that ducks were not allowed on buses, but, when my aunt asked to see written evidence of this, he could not produce any. So he let her take them on board. My aunt shouted at the boys to leave her feathered friends alone when they all crowded round and wanted to pet them and everyone had a good laugh – except for the poor harassed conductor who was trying to restore order.

This was the start of it all.

Next, Aunt Lillian took the ducks into the village post office and unfortunately they did several little 'whoopsies' on the floor whilst they were waiting in the queue. The Vicar, who had just purchased a postal order and was not looking where he was going, slipped on the offending mess and very nearly went head over heels. Aunt Lillian told me it was all the fault of the other customers and the staff who started shouting and telling her to leave. She explained that Pip, Squeak and Wilfred were scared, and when they were scared they had little accidents. If everyone had stayed calm, she and her pets would have gone up to the counter, been served and left without incident.

"Anyway, I don't know what you are worried about," she chided me. "We have been practising going out over the past few days and they are now little angels."

The ducks quacked gently and looked up at us, as if to say: "We are not going to be any trouble at all. We know how to behave ourselves." I was not so sure. Ducks can be very tricky creatures and these three were no exception. They could be trouble, and I was sure that they had that look in their eyes.

I knew there was no point in arguing with my aunt when she had her mind set on something, so I declared with some reluctance: "OK, we had better hurry as we do not want to go in late. You know how that annoys the Vicar's wife." Arriving after the choir was a 'no, no.'

So we set off across the village green and just happened to arrive at the same time as Mrs Goss, the Vicar's wife. I could see by the horrified look on her face that she was not happy.

"What are those?" she demanded, pointing to the ducks.

"Isn't it quite obvious, Mrs Goss — those are ducks," my aunt replied with a very straight face, and I started to giggle.

"I can see they are ducks, Mrs Auger, but where are you going with them?"

"Again, I would have thought that was obvious," said Aunt Lillian, somewhat peevishly. "I am going into church to listen to your husband preach, and take part in the Harvest Festival. Jojo here has our contribution of some apples from the garden. Nice eaters they are, so I am sure you will enjoy them when you take them home."

I could hear that she was being sarcastic, but Mrs Goss seemed unaware of the jibe.

"Animals are not allowed in church." She could be quite a bossy woman and my aunt did not like her one little bit.

Aunt Lillian countered with the argument: "Ducks are

not animals, but birds. They are on leads and surely, as God's creatures, they will be welcomed into the arms of the church."

By now the Vicar's wife should have beaten a hasty retreat as I knew she was no match for my aunt in full flow. The argument continued to get more heated until the arrival of the Vicar and choir.

Eleven o'clock had struck and the service was now running late. The congregation were becoming restless as they wanted to get home for Sunday lunch or to the pub for a quick half before returning to the bosom of their families. The level of noise from inside the church was steadily growing.

By this time I had wandered off to read the notices in the porch and saw that the Vicar and my aunt were talking – heated words were exchanged and eventually a compromise seemed to be reached.

As the organ struck up the Introit and the Vicar started to lead the choir to their places, I waited with bated breath to see what Aunt Lillian would do. I knew it was too much to expect that she had been persuaded to leave the ducks outside or to sit at the back, but I suspected this was what the poor Vicar thought he had agreed.

She looked at me and whispered: "Come on, Jojo, we will go in now, following the choir, and nobody will notice us."

"Can't we just sit here in the back row?" I pointed hopefully to a seat, slipping into the last row of pews, but deep down I knew my plea would be ignored. There was no stopping my aunt. There she was, bringing up the rear of the procession, followed by the ducks, who were all kitted out with their Sunday best bow ties around their necks, and very dapper they looked too.

My aunt, smartly dressed with a jaunty little hat and umbrella with a duck handle, was smiling broadly. Smugly she marched down the aisle to take her place in the front pew, with the ducks waddling after her, trying to keep up and leaving 'little parcels' on the way.

The congregation were all trying to see what was happening. They knew that Mrs Auger was always good entertainment, and whispers were going round the church that today something was going to happen.

The Vicar, from the front of the church, was waving her back and getting very red in the face. "Mrs Auger, we agreed that you would leave them tied up to the boot scraper," he said.

"No, you agreed – I did not, and anyway, someone might steal them." Lillian was obviously not keeping to her side of the bargain and she pretended not to understand when the Vicar pointed to the door.

She sat down, composed herself and drew the ducks into the space under the pew. To add insult to injury, she looked up expectantly, and then impatiently signed for the flustered minister to proceed.

I shrank down into my seat, hoping that she would forget that I was with her, and for a moment I thought I had succeeded, as the door opened once again. Unfortunately, the Vicar's wife had waited to compose herself after the contretemps, and as she rushed up to take her seat she slipped on the ducks' droppings and fell down with a crash.

Suppressed laughter was heard, which only made things worse. The choir could not contain themselves and the Vicar rushed down to help his hapless wife. She burst into tears and rushed out, followed by her husband.

The congregation looked at one another and did not know what to do. The organ played 'All Things Bright and Beautiful' at full blast, as the organist could not see what was happening. The young choirboys were quite beside themselves with mirth, and chaos reigned.

We all waited and waited, but nothing happened. So after a while people began to wander out; others gathered to gossip and catch up on the news. This incident would grow with the telling and my mother would have to face more embarrassment.

Lillian just sat in the front row looking quite angelic, not moving a muscle, but humming her favourite hymn quietly to herself. Her gaze was on the crucified Christ and she ignored all the confusion around her.

The church became empty and we just sat there. The three ducks had gone to sleep under the seat and silence reigned. After about five minutes of deep meditation, my aunt turned to me and said: "I don't suppose there is any point waiting here. I think the service must have been cancelled."

Somehow Aunt Lillian always seemed to be unaware that she was the cause of the pandemonium around her. I must say she was never a boring person to go out with, unlike some of my other relations, and, as a child, I was not always fully aware of the problems she caused. I just found her a really interesting, albeit often embarrassing, companion.

## CHAPTER 13

# Crying Wolf!

"I am really going to die this time," Aunt Lillian whimpered as I entered the kitchen. "There is no doubt about it. You will all be sorry when I am gone. Remember me kindly, Jojo."

Our whole family had heard this on so many occasions that we tended to ignore these frantic cries for help.

"Jojo, can you run round and ask Dr. Goulston to call, as soon as possible?" she asked, flopping down into a chair and putting her head in her hands.

"Why, what is the matter this time?" I enquired, quite resigned to the fact that this was going to be another false alarm. "Let me put the kettle on and get you a nice cup of tea. That will make you feel better."

"Time is of the essence," my aunt insisted. "We don't have time for a cup of tea. Get the doctor now or you will regret the fact that you let your old aunt die in agony."

My aunt always loved to be dramatic and she was quite well known for her bravura performances when she wanted to get her own way.

"It would be better if I ask Mum to come round," I

said. "You know Dr. Goulston threatened to blacklist you because you kept calling him out on false alarms, and you are now running out of options. Dr. Morrisey took you off his books last year, and you only managed to get on Dr. Goulston's list by threatening to go to the local paper."

I sat myself down at the kitchen table as I knew this was going to result in a long debate.

"All doctors are the same," lamented Aunt Lillian, taking off her glasses and rubbing her eyes. "They sell snake oil remedies and then they are surprised when people die under their care. You can't trust doctors, you know."

"Then why do you want me to go and get the doctor if you don't think they are any good?" I enquired as I walked to the sink to fill the kettle.

"Because I'm desperate!" came the reply. "Do I look like a well person to you? Come over here and look in my eyes." She pulled down the bottom lid of her right eye. "Are my eyes turning blue?"

It was always easier to go along with her at times, so I walked over and looked into her eyes.

"Are they turning blue?" she demanded, grabbing my sleeve. "Look carefully."

"No, your eyes are a greeny-grey colour," I said, turning back towards the sink.

"Greeny-grey, you say. That sounds just as bad, but I really thought they would be turning blue by now. This is an emergency. Don't just stand there. Do something!"

I was getting a bit bored with all this talk so I picked up my coat, which I had flung onto the chair, and put it on. "I'll get Mum. She always knows what to do in an emergency." I walked towards the door.

"No, don't get her," bellowed my aunt. "She will wait until I expire here on the kitchen floor. She is just waiting to get her hands on this house. I can see that by the way she looks around each time she comes over. She is weighing up how much everything is worth and where she is going to put her furniture. I know what your mother is like, Jojo; you have to do something now. You must run and get the doctor. My very life depends on it."

"But Auntie… ", I trailed off because she had perked up somewhat. "You look fine to me. What is the matter with you, anyway? If I go for the doctor he is bound to ask me."

"I can't tell you," she whispered. "You are only a child and it's personal."

"Oh, a 'woman's thing', is it?" I asked. I knew women had problems they could not talk about and when I asked about them I was told "Hush, it's a 'woman's thing'." This certainly piqued my curiosity. I remembered that I had got a clip round the ear once for stating that I would grow up to be a woman one day so I should know about such things. I certainly didn't want to be caught out by 'women's things'.

"No," my aunt said firmly. "It is not anything to do

with women's things, but it is certainly not something I would discuss with a child like you." She drew herself up somewhat and now looked fully restored to health.

"Well, if it isn't 'women's things' then you can surely tell me," I persisted. "I know it can't be 'men's things' because nobody ever seems to have them, and you are a woman after all." I felt quite proud of my logical argument.

Aunt Lillian slumped back down into her chair. "Why have I got such an argumentative niece? You could die in this house waiting for medical help."

At that moment I noticed she was clasping something in her hand that she had taken out of her apron pocket.

"What's that you are holding?" I asked.

She quickly hid it away under the table. "That is the problem and that is how I know I am really going to die this time," she muttered. "If you don't hurry and get help you may be left here with a dead body on your hands and then you will be sorry."

I was now getting a bit concerned. I had never seen a dead body before. Perhaps the police would come and think that I had murdered her. They might drag me down to the police station and torture me to get a confession. I had been learning about the Tower of London at school and the way they used thumb-screws and sometimes the rack in the olden days to extract confessions, sometimes from people that were innocent. I shuddered at the thought and started towards the door. I ran down the lane and across Golden Acre towards St. John's Church. Dr.

Goulston's surgery was next door to the church and I was quite out of breath by the time I got there. I went round to the back door and knocked loudly several times.

"Okay, okay, I'm coming. What's the matter?" a voice shouted. "Has the Black Death reached the village?"

The door opened wide and Dr. Goulston stood there. "Oh, it's you, Jojo," he sighed. "What's happened this time? Don't tell me, your aunt wants me to drop everything I am doing and rush round to save her life."

"How did you guess doctor?" I was quite surprised that he knew why I was there. "Are you a wizard or something, or do you have second sight?"

"No, Jojo, I don't have to be psychic to know that when you come knocking on my door quite out of breath, it is about your aunt."

"Well, you are right," I confirmed. "This time she says she really is going to die and I don't want to stay in the house with her while she dies because the police might think I had done her in." I jumped from foot to foot. "Please come and see her."

"I am busy right now, but go back and tell her I will call round at the end of surgery this morning," he said. "I'll be there about eleven o'clock. Tell her to hang on until then." With that, he closed the door, and there was nothing else I could do, so I turned back towards my aunt's house.

I wondered if I should go and get Mum. I knew she would not be best pleased if I called her away on baking day, especially if it was a fool's errand and there was nothing wrong with my aunt.

As I walked I saw Neville climbing up a tree and went over to talk to him.

"What's the matter, Jojo? You look really worried," he said.

"I am, Aunt Lillian tells me that she is going to die and the doctor can't come straight away," I told him.

"Gosh!" he responded. "Can I come and watch her die? I have never seen anyone die before and I want to be a doctor when I grow up, so it would be a good experience for me." He started to climb down and ran ahead of me towards Aunt Lillian's house.

"No, you can't come and watch her die," I yelled. "Think of it, Neville. You could be had up as an accomplice and taken away by the secret police. They might put you in a cell and throw away the key."

This stopped him in his tracks. "I hadn't thought of that," he mused. "Do all doctors get taken to the police station when they find dead bodies?"

"I don't think so," I said. "But you're not a doctor. Anyway you can come with me if you like, as I would not mind some company going back there."

"Come on, then." He pulled my arm. "We might just get there in time if we hurry." We ran back to the house together.

"Where is the doctor, and why is he here?" Aunt Lillian shouted, pointing at Neville as we entered the kitchen.

"Neville asked if he could come and watch you die, because he wants to be a doctor when he grows up," I explained.

"This is not a freak show at the fair, you know," my aunt scolded, sitting up straight and peering over her glasses which had slipped down her nose. "Dying is a serious business."

I could see that poor Neville wished he had not asked to come. He shrank back into the corner.

"What is in this bottle?" I asked, picking up a bottle from the table and looking at it closely. "It is bright blue. Is it a new drink or something?"

"Give me that, here," snapped my aunt, snatching it from me. "It is not a drink – it is personal."

At that moment the back door flew open and my Aunt Avis came in. She was Aunt Lillian's daughter and was always in a rush. She blew in and blew out all the time like a whirlwind rushing through the house.

"Hi, Mum" she called. "How are you? Did you like the surprise I left for you?"

Aunt Lillian quickly went back into sick mode. She sat at the table and just managed a pathetic stage whisper: "Thank goodness you have come, Avis. You have arrived in the nick of time, I am dying and this stupid child" – she pointed at me – "went to get the doctor, but brought back her friend Neville, who wants to watch me die. Horrid child that he is. What is the matter with children these days?"

"Well, what is the matter with you Mum?" asked Avis, concerned, pushing back a strand of hair which had fallen over her sparkling blue eyes.

"No, I can't tell you in front of them. It is personal," Aunt Lillian insisted.

"It's not a 'woman's thing'," I told her, "nor a man's thing either, but I think it has something to do with this." I held up the bottle of blue liquid.

"Where did you get that, Jojo?" Aunt Avis wanted to know.

"Auntie was trying to hide it in her apron pocket," I explained.

"Give it to me" shouted Aunt Lillian. "It is a sample and I want the doctor to look at it when he eventually arrives. Hopefully I will live long enough for him to find an antidote."

"A sample of what?" Aunt Avis demanded.

"You know what. It's a sample," Aunt Lillian hissed. Obviously forgetting that we were both there, she continued: "It's a sample of my pee. When I went to the lavatory this morning, that was the colour it was, so I took a sample to give to the doctor. You see, I am really dying because nobody has pee that colour."

Neville leapt forward, forgetting he was trying to fade into the background. "Can I look? I am going to be a doctor when I grow up and I would like to see blue pee," he said excitedly.

"Well, you can certainly look at this, Neville, because

it is not pee at all," Aunt Avis told him, and burst out laughing.

"How dare you laugh at an old lady when she is dying of a strange tropical disease," Aunt Lillian yelled, rising up to her full five foot.

"Mum, you are not dying at all," her daughter spluttered, tears of laughter running down her cheeks. "There is nothing wrong with you. I know exactly what that is."

"How can you possibly tell – you are not a trained doctor," Lillian exclaimed. "I know when I am dying."

"We will all die one day, but this is not your moment to go to the Almighty," said Avis, drying her eyes. "I put a new cleaner in the toilet when I was here yesterday and I forgot to tell you. It was one of those Bloo-loo products that you put in the cistern and, when you flush, it foams up and cleans the toilet. I thought it would save you another job, as you are always moaning about housework."

"So I am not going to die then?" gasped Lillian. Jumping up from her chair, she grabbed the kettle and rushed over to the sink.

"No, you will live to fight another day."

Just then there was a knock at the door. Silence fell and Aunt Lillian went a delicate shade of pink.

"That must be the doctor," I cried out.

"Go and tell him it was all a mistake, Jojo," Aunt Lillian instructed. "You must have misheard me. I never asked you to go to get the doctor. I knew what it was all the time," she added sheepishly, "otherwise, it will get round the whole village and I will be a laughing stock."

"You go and do your own dirty work," laughed Avis. "You got yourself into this, so you have to get yourself out of it. That will teach you not to cry wolf the next time."

# CHAPTER 14

# Wonkey Donkey Gets an Airing

August meant Cricket Week in our village, which gave us kids the chance to enter a fancy dress competition, and we wanted to do something really different this year.

"How about using our soap box carts?" I suggested. "We could decorate the carts to match the characters we dress up as, and follow behind the main procession. That should make an impression on the judges."

We sat around under the tree in Aunt Lillian's garden giving it great thought. Suddenly Mikey, my brother, jumped up and declared: "I know, I am going to be a Roman soldier and make my cart into a chariot, just like I saw in the film *Ben-Hur*. I will stick knives on the wheels and kill the Barbarians. They will rue the day that they tangled with me."

"You won't make a very convincing Roman because you hate to go fast and anyway, there are no Barbarians around here," I said quite derisively, "and there's no way Mum will let you put knives on the wheels."

I was not particularly fond of my brother. He was always getting both of us into trouble because he always looked so guilty when we had done something wrong. Mum would pump him for information, and even though she did not physically hurt him, he would give the game away. He was a bit of a wimpy kid.

After a great deal of discussion and ideas being mooted and rejected, I made my choice. "I am going to be Boadicea," I announced. "I will stand in the back of my chariot and fight for my tribe." I picked up the garden rake and stood in a pose like Britannia on the back of the penny. "Everyone will cheer for me and I will win first prize." I was always full of my own importance, even then.

"Who are you going to be, Neville?" I asked. Neville always trailed along behind us and sometimes we let him join in our games, so that we had someone we could beat. But he was very brainy and came up with grand ideas.

"Well, we are learning about the Egyptians at school," he whispered. "Perhaps I will be Ramses – he turned into a god, you know." He was now getting into his stride. "I will ride in my war chariot against the Assyrians – or perhaps I will be an Assyrian because they must have been really strong as they rode down like a wolf on the fold and that sounds exciting. Err… that's if you'll let me join in."

Like all small children, we could be quite cruel and none of us could imagine Neville fighting with anyone. He was a really skinny kid, who had little national health glasses perched on the end of his nose, and peered at everyone like a mole tunnelling into the light.

He came from the wrong side of the tracks in our village, and wore patched trousers and a jumper with holes in the sleeves, which always had a long line of snot trailing up towards his elbows. Neville's personal hygiene left a lot to be desired and only the previous day Nurse Nora had found nits in his hair, which had resulted in her shaving his head.

Mum said that we should not play with him, but he was a particular favourite of my Aunt Lillian. She invited him round to her house and told us that we should play with him because he needed some friends.

Suddenly my aunt's voice shouted: "Who wants some home-made lemonade? I have also just baked a batch of biscuits?"

We said 'yes' to the lemonade, but wanted to know what was in the biscuits because we had become quite wary of my aunt's cooking. She could be very creative with flavours. Only last week she had made a special sherry trifle with sherry vinegar soaked sponge and tinned plum tomatoes instead of plums. That had not gone down very well at a family gathering.

Aunt Lillian also managed to muddle sugar and salt on various occasions, to the detrimental effect on her culinary skills. So we always asked about the ingredients, then smelt the product and tasted a little bit to begin with. You just never knew what you were going to get. It was always good or bad, never indifferent, and this was all before the age of Heston Blumenthal and his creative ideas.

My aunt came across to us carrying a tray and exclaimed: "Well, help yourselves, then. Don't expect me to serve you all. Anyway, what did your last slave die of? It was certainly not idleness." This was one of her favourite sayings.

I tentatively picked up one of the biscuits. I must say, it looked as though she had collected up the bluebottles that occasionally gathered round the dog's bowl, then squashed them and sandwiched them between biscuits. "What did you put in these? Do they have a name?"

"Yes, they do, Miss Smarty-pants. They are called Garibaldi Biscuits, and in case you didn't realise, I purchased them in Pearce's, the grocers in the village. He told me that they were a new line he was trying out. So there! Go on, try them."

"Are you sure that you bought them and did not make them?" I persisted. "They do look like they are made of dead flies."

"I don't mind trying them, Mrs Auger," piped up Neville. He always was a bit of a creep where my aunt was concerned.

"Well, what have you kids been up to all morning?" Aunt Lillian asked.

"It is Cricket Week and Saturday is the fancy dress

parade," I reminded her. "We have been thinking about what we are going to go as."

"What have you decided?"

"We are going to make our soap boxes into chariots and go as famous people. I will be Boadicea, Mikey fancies himself as Ben Hur and Neville is going to be an Assyrian – whoever he was."

"What a fantastic idea," Aunt Lillian enthused. "Can I join in? I know what I would go as."

"No, you can't!" we all shouted. We had been embarrassed by my aunt's antics in the past and wanted to distance ourselves a bit. "Anyway, you don't have a soap box so you can't join in with us," I told her, trying to let her down gently.

"Well, I can build one," she insisted. "There is an old pram in the shed and I will get young Trevor to put that orange box on the back – then Bob's your uncle and Fanny's your aunt. I will have a soap box to rival any kid in the village. What do you think?"

We all looked at one another, but none of us quite had the nerve to tell her what we thought.

She rushed over to the shed, flung open the door and dragged a very dilapidated pram out onto the lawn. The pram had been nick-named 'Wonkey Donkey' because the wheels did not go round properly.

My aunt was now in full cry. "If I can't make it into a soap box, I will get one of you to push me in this contraption. I am going as Penny for the Guy."

We laughed and pointed out that Penny for the Guy was not until November, another three months away, but she had an answer to that.

"You will all be laughing on the other side of your faces when I get people to give me contributions this early in the year," she said. "We'll be able to have a super bonfire party in November because we will have lots of money to buy rockets, Catherine wheels and loads of sparklers. It is always the early bird that catches the worm.

"Or perhaps I could go as a baby and wear a nappy, with a bonnet on my head and a dummy in my mouth. I could look quite the part and people would be really fooled."

Bearing in mind that she was not quite five foot tall and weighed in at less than seven stone, we could quite picture her as either.

"What do you think? Which is it going to be – guy or baby?"

"I think you would be a really good baby," I said. "Why don't we give it a try first and if we don't like it you can become a guy."

"Jojo, you are a genius. When it comes to brains, you are certainly your aunt's nephew."

"Don't you mean niece?" I queried. "I am a girl, you know."

"Well, whatever. I will go in to get changed for the part, and then you can push me down the village. We will take a straw poll of village opinion."

After a short time Aunt Lillian reappeared, wearing a long white nightdress and pink woollen bed socks. The outfit was topped off with a floral bonnet, which had a large wide brim.

"I thought you were going to wear a nappy," I said.

"I will have you know that I am." She proceeded to lift up the hem of the nightie and, lo and behold, she had a towel wrapped around her with a big safety pin at the front. She also had her long pink drawers on under it and looked quite a sight, I can tell you.

"I could not find a dummy, so I will just put my thumb in my mouth instead," she informed us. "Come on, you lot. Off we go." She promptly jumped into the pram and sat there with her thumb in her mouth.

We set off pushing her down the lane towards the village green, and luckily nobody saw us on the way.

However, this was to change. "Go via the butcher," Aunt Lillian instructed. "I can then get a couple of chops for tea and that will kill two birds with one stone."

We kids just loved getting involved in these escapades and pushed her quickly over the green to the top of the hill leading down to the mill pond.

This was when disaster struck. We each thought that the other one was holding the pram handle, when we spied Mrs Jones with her new puppy and went over to stroke it.

Suddenly there was a terrible screech, scream and shout. We looked at each other in horror, when we realised that the screaming was coming from Aunt Lillian as she careered down the hill at ever increasing speed.

"Stop!" we shouted in unison to no one in particular. "Stop that pram."

Unfortunately the Vicar was walking up the hill and, because he was very short sighted, he strode into the path of the oncoming pram. It hit him full on and he was bowled over.

Then the blacksmith saw what was happening and ran after the pram, shouting: "I will save that child. Stand back everyone."

By now the pram had reached the edge of the pond and stopped of its own accord, only to be propelled out into the depths of the water by the blacksmith, who had tripped on the kerb.

There was a big splash, but the blacksmith was up immediately. He jumped into the pond and grabbed the 'baby' before running back to the shore.

"Put me down this minute, young man," protested my aunt. "What do you think you are up to?"

The startled blacksmith now realised his mistake, and dropped Aunt Lillian back into the shallows.

"Why did you drop me back into the water? Are you stupid or something?" she demanded.

"I thought you were a child in need of rescue," he spluttered.

"Of course, I am not a child. I am a fully grown woman, and now I am soaked right through. Pull me up this instance," she commanded and held out her hand.

"If I had known it was you I would have let you stay in the water," he muttered, but he held out his hand and pulled her upright. It was then that the water-soaked nappy fell around her ankles.

Quite a crowd had gathered to see what all the noise was about and everyone burst out laughing.

Aunt Lillian could always see the funny side of most situations, even if she was the butt of the joke. But her practical side took over. "Jojo," she shouted, "take your shoes and socks off and get the pram for me."

I waded in and pulled out 'Wonkey Donkey' and we made our way home.

We were certain that Aunt Lillian would not be going to the fancy dress parade as a baby in a pram until she commented: "Well, that went rather well, I think. It certainly made people sit up and take notice."

CHAPTER 15

# Bring Out Your Dead

My Aunt Lillian loved a good funeral and would often join the congregation in the local church if some big-wig was being buried. She kept an eye on the church notices throughout the whole parish.

She would always tell me: "Jojo, you get better food at the wake of a big shot and large schooners of sherry, not tiny thimbles that the lower classes provide. There are always lots of people, so you can mingle and not be noticed."

She did not add that she had been thrown out several times when she got tiddly and started to criticise the upper classes in general, or refer to the faults of the deceased.

When I arrived at her house I noticed that she was dressed in black and looking very down in the mouth.

"Lucky is dead," she informed me sombrely. "He passed away last night and has gone to live with Jesus in the big cats' home in the sky. I found him lying in the garden this morning, with his four paws sticking up towards heaven as if trying to get there."

I had always thought that Lucky was not a good name

for that cat as he had used up so many of his lives while living with her. Obviously, nine lives had not been enough and he had got his comeuppance.

"Do you want to view the body?" she asked. "If you do, come this way." She led me into the conservatory like an old fashioned undertaker and drew back the sheet with a flourish. There lay Lucky, stretched out on a cushion, and I must say he looked very peaceful, as though he was just lying in the sun and dreaming of catching mice.

"What are you going to do with him? Are you going to bury him in the back garden?" I asked. "If so, can I invite my friends round, like we usually do, and have a proper funeral?"

My aunt certainly knew how to put on a spread, and my friends were always up for attending her burial services. They would bring any dead animals, insects or fish to her, and I sometimes thought that the boys might have killed them just to have the opportunity of being part of the ceremonies. Dead moths, caterpillars, spiders and goldfish were brought to her house. She never disappointed us and her garden contained a graveyard, with little crosses that looked like the battlefield of Flanders.

"I am going to give Lucky a big send off – his funeral is going to become the centre of my advertising campaign," she replied, her eyes twinkling behind her glasses. "You can be the pall bearer. We will dress you up like an angel, with flowers in your hair, and we can put

him in a little coffin which you can carry to the graveside, with tears running gently down your cheeks."

"What advertising campaign are you talking about?
Advertising what?" I questioned, fearing that Aunt Lillian
was going to involve me in another of her mad cap
schemes.

She patted me on the head and mused: "You will look beautiful, and we will invite the Press round to take pictures. You will make the front page of the local paper and this will launch my new venture. Lucky's death, tragic as it is, gave me a wonderful idea."

Drama was always Aunt Lillian's forte and she really should have gone on the stage.

"What idea is that?" I asked tentatively. Ideas and my aunt were a combination that always spelled trouble and it was usually trouble for the person who was fool enough to get involved. I had been known to take part in her schemes in the past and I had always lived to regret it. Somehow I never seemed to learn and I could see another load of trouble heading my way.

"Funerals for pets is going to be big business and we are going to get in first, before anyone steals my idea," Aunt Lillian enthused. "Do you know how many animals there are in this village alone? There are cats, dogs, sheep, cows, pigs and budgerigars to name but a few, and people from the surrounding area will soon be flocking here to take advantage of our services."

I could see she was getting carried away as usual, and I was grateful that a circus was not in town. I wondered how we could possibly find a box big enough to take an elephant if it popped its clogs – let alone manoeuvre it into the grave. How many pall bearers would that require? More than just me dressed as an angel or whatever character she came up with.

I suspected that if we were asked to bury a sheep I would have to dress as Little Bo Peep or something equally ridiculous – and who was going to dig the holes? We were certainly not the proud owners of a mechanical digger and I had a horrible feeling that the job would also fall to me. I did not see myself as a grave digger extraordinaire.

There was no stopping her now she was in full flow. "You could go around the village with a bell, shouting 'Bring out your dead!' in your loudest voice. You'd collect the bodies on your go-cart and bring them back here for burial at the bottom of the garden."

"Wasn't that what they did for plague victims?" I scoffed. "I really don't think that the Black Death is going to return in the near future, and my go-cart wouldn't be able to carry a pig or a cow."

"Don't be so negative, Jojo," she replied, undaunted. "Multi-national corporations were not created on negativity. You must have a positive approach to build a business empire. We will print flyers and you can distribute them around the neighbourhood to drum up business. Word of mouth will then kick in.

"I think it is a grand plan. When it becomes too big for us to handle we can franchise the idea, sit back and become millionaires. What do you think of that?"

Personally I did not think much of it, and to bring her back to earth I pointed down at the body lying between us. "In the mean time, what are we going to do with Lucky?"

"Lucky will be our launch pad. We have to start somewhere and there is no time like the present." With this, she whisked a shoe box out from under the table.

I must point out that my aunt wore size two shoes and Lucky had been a well-fed cat who had regularly supplemented his diet with birds, shrews and mice.

"No way is he going to fit in there!" I exclaimed.

"We could fold him up small and then tie the lid on tight so that he does not pop out."

She picked Lucky up and held him over the box. "Uh-mm, perhaps I will have to think of something else. I did not realise that he had grown so big. No wonder he cost so much to feed."

"How about that basket?" I queried, pointing to a wicker basket in the corner. "It has been lying there for ages and would make a great coffin."

Lucky was promptly stuffed unceremoniously into the basket and folded up like a concertina, but his little black paws still stuck up over the top.

"I think rigour mortis must have set in," she said as she tried to bend them to fit. "I know it wears off after a while and then we will be able to fit him in there, snug as a bug in a rug. Before I forget, I must telephone Trevor to ask him if he can dig the grave for me."

By eleven o'clock on the following day nine of my school friends were gathered in the garden. We were told to line up in twos and follow Aunt Lillian to the graveside. She was dressed in a black lace frock, a long black cardigan that had been darned at the elbows with bright red wool and a rather attractive black hat, with a bright yellow feather, perched on her head at a jaunty angle.

I followed her, dressed in my best white dress, with a daisy chain looped through my hair which kept flopping down over my eyes and making me stumble. I was carrying Lucky in the basket that was tied up with a rather fetching pink bow and was anxious not to drop him.

All the kids were dolled up in various items of clothing, reminiscent of a rummage in the dressing up box. What a motley crew we looked.

"Come this way children, spread out and make room for everyone," ordered my aunt.

Our eleven-strong congregation stood around a hole big enough to bury a lion in because Trevor had got carried away with his task — over compensation must run in our family — and Aunt Lillian opened the Book of Common Prayer.

We kids sang 'Onward Christian Soldiers', one of my aunt's favourites, and we all knew the words from school assembly. We were somewhat off-key, but enthusiasm made up for musical content.

"Dust to dust and ashes to ashes in the sure and certain… " she declaimed. She just loved the drama of this speech, but was cut off in mid flow by a piercing scream as Neville slipped and fell into the hole. It was so deep that we could only see the top of his head. He started to wail loudly.

"Well," said Aunt Lillian, looking down on him, "it is certainly deep enough."

We all giggled as Neville was yanked out and promised extra rations at the party to stop him crying. He stood there shivering and snivelling with a candle of snot running down his top lip which he proceeded to wipe on his sleeve.

Poor Neville had yellow mud all over this face and hands. This was smeared onto his sleeve as well, and he looked like a soldier in camouflage mode.

Without further ado, Lucky was lowered into the earth and we threw daisies in on top of the basket, eager to get to the important part of the proceedings. I knew that a spread was laid out under the apple tree – plus watered down Council orange juice (this was handed out after the war to give children extra Vitamin C).

There were slabs of bread pudding and Lincoln biscuits with the dots on that we nibbled round and round, racing each other to reach the centre first. We were not allowed to do this at home as it was considered bad manners, but my aunt never seemed to mind and joined in with great gusto. She was, however, quite miffed if someone beat her.

When the party was over, the kids began to leave, but by this time people from the village had begun to gather round the notice pinned to the tree by the front gate which said:

## Pet Funerals
*No animal too big or too small.*
*Services conducted with great decorum.*
*Enquire Within.*

Some tutting was heard and a few people shook their heads, while others made comments like "Old Mother Auger is up to her antics again. What will she think of next?"

As the crowd grew laughing broke out.

Aunt Lillian just smiled: "See, people are beginning to notice already. I knew this idea would be a winner. Just you wait and see, Jojo."

Suddenly Mrs Parslow, the farmer's wife, stepped forward from the group. She called out: "Mrs Auger, my husband has a problem and your new business is just the answer." She turned back towards her group of cronies and grinned.

"I told you this was the way forward," Aunt Lillian whispered to me. Turning to Mrs Parslow, she chirped: "How may I be of assistance to your husband?"

I could tell that she was trying to impress because she was using her really posh voice.

"Well," said Mrs Parslow, a plump lady with a round face and big, red cheeks, "the vet has just put down Daisy, his favourite milker, and my husband does not want to send her off for dog meat. Sentimental old fool I say, but he will not change after all these years. It is his birthday in a couple of days and, seeing your notice, I thought I would arrange for you to give Daisy a good send off as a birthday present."

I was horrified. I knew that Daisy was a huge cow, and I tried to get my aunt's attention, but there was no stopping her.

"We would be delighted to help," she said. "If you would come into the kitchen we can book a slot in the diary and I can take down the details of the order of service you would like. We offer many different types of ceremonies, and Jojo can dress as a milkmaid to follow the coffin. It will be quite magnificent and just the send-off for a favourite cow."

She continued her sales-pitch in the kitchen where I wriggled around on my seat in frustration.

"Surely it would be easier for Mr Parslow to bury Daisy on the farm," I blurted out.

"Shush. What is the matter with you, Jojo?" admonished my aunt. "Have you got ants in your pants or something? If you are not going to act in a businesslike manner then I suggest that you leave us grown-ups to it." Turning back to Mrs Parslow, she added: "Children should be seen and not heard, I always say! Now, where were we?"

"Burying Daisy," said Mrs Parslow.

"Oh, yes. How about next Friday at 11a.m? The local kids are on holiday and they can act as pall bearers. Jojo will get her friends to do it."

I had visions of my friends trying to carry a huge

coffin containing the cow and crumpling under the weight.

"We can't do that!" I cried. "Do you have any idea how much a cow weighs?"

By this time four of Mrs Parslow's friends had joined us in the kitchen and giggling broke out.

Mrs Parslow said with a smile: "I was only joking. As Jojo says, it will be much easier for Bill to bury Daisy on the farm."

After this they left and my aunt turned angrily to me. "What did you say that for? You lost a sale and that is unforgivable in business. If you can't say anything positive then you should shut up."

I tried to look repentant, but was secretly relieved that I had averted another disaster. I knew it would be today's topic of village gossip and my mother would not be happy, but I had a clear conscience.

Some eccentric people are loved for their strangeness and this summed up my aunt perfectly.

CHAPTER 16

# Christmas is Cancelled This Year!

I was skipping down the path singing 'Jingle Bells' at the top of my voice. It was only three days until Christmas and I was now getting excited. My letter had been sent to Santa Claus, informing him how good I had been and how much I would like the new bike I had seen in the shop in the High Street. I thought it was a good omen that sixteen fire fairies grabbed the letter when we set fire to it in the grate. I knew they would take my request directly to the elves, and Santa would pack the bright blue bicycle onto his sleigh, with my name on the gift tag.

Christmas was a big event in our family and everyone got together to share in the fun. Mum always bought the biggest turkey, and we had crackers, with jokes and party hats, plus Christmas pudding with holly on it. Everyone came to our house to tuck into mince pies and sausage rolls, trifle, jelly and fruit salad, all laid out for tea. We all ate too much!

So I was very surprised when I visited Aunt Lillian and

was immediately informed by her: "I want no part of Christmas this year."

My mouth dropped open in disbelief as she went on: "I have decided to become a vegetarian. I know that Christmas falls at the time of the pagan festival celebrating the Solstice and that is when they killed animals to salt them for the coming winter. I want no part of that. It is just a bloodfest… "

"What is a bloodfest?" I asked. It sounded pretty horrid to me, not at all like Christmas as I knew it.

"A bloodfest is when they slit the throats of the animals and drain all the blood out," my aunt explained. "Then people paint themselves with the blood and sing pagan songs around a bonfire."

Knowing that she always dramatised things, I argued: "I don't think that happens in our village. I have never seen anyone covered in blood or heard any pagan songs. The only songs I've heard so far have been from the carol singers, who came round last night collecting money for the starving babies in Africa."

"Perhaps they were pagans in disguise," she teased me, her eyes twinkling behind her spectacles. "I bet you never thought of that. They are everywhere, you know, just waiting to practise their rites when the moon is full and the Solstice comes around. That is why I will not be celebrating Christmas this year."

"Don't say that," I pleaded. "You always come to our house for Christmas lunch and then we play games and open our presents. There are lots under the tree already, and I am sure there are some with your name on them."

"Well, you can tell your mother that I will not be coming this year," Aunt Lillian insisted. "I won't be sending Christmas cards either, and I don't want any presents, because it has become a Feast of Beelzebub and has lost the spirit of God's birthday."

I had been so shocked by her outburst that I had become rooted to the spot and left the kitchen door open.

"Don't just stand there," she instructed. "Come in and close the door – you are letting all the cold air into the kitchen." She stamped over to the sink, looking quite sulky.

I shut the door and walked over to the kitchen table. "It's Jesus' birthday – not God's birthday at Christmas," I pointed out. "Our Sunday School teacher told me that. Jesus' birthday falls on December 25th, but God has his birthday every day."

"Well, whoever's birthday it is, I will not be celebrating it," Aunt Lillian replied, clearly in one of her moods.

She had always been the life and soul of the party and I knew we kids would miss her. I was not sure that my mother would be sorry, but I knew I would be. Aunt Lillian played lots of songs on the piano and always joined in the party games. Musical chairs and pass the parcel would not be the same without her. I was getting really worried now. Other adults in our family did not participate in the festivities in the same way as my aunt did, so the day would lose its special sparkle.

Glancing out of the window I shouted excitedly: "Look, it has just started to snow and I think we will have a white Christmas. If you aren't coming over to our house, who is going to help us build the snowman? Who will light the candles on the tree?" I could see it now; we would all be sitting around, just looking at each other. My aunt was always the one who came up with ideas to get things going.

At that point the kettle began to sing and my aunt bustled around making some tea. "Help yourself to one of my mince pies, I have just taken them out of the oven, so be careful, they are hot."

I quickly declined. My aunt was not a very good cook, but she was certainly an inventive one when it came to baking. She had once made dainty little pies and filled them with Kitty Kat by mistake, so I was now wary of eating anything she had cooked.

I drank my tea while still in shock over her decision not to join in the festivities, and then went home to break the news to Mum.

Mother was not surprised, and informed us that this time she would call Aunt Lillian's bluff by letting everyone know that she had 'cancelled Christmas'. We didn't send any Christmas cards to her and, as I usually made my own cards, that was one less that needed colouring in. We put up paper chains and decorated the tree, while the pile of presents began to increase. I kept creeping in to see how many had my name on them. There was no bike, but perhaps that was being delivered on Christmas morning. What was worrying was that it would not go into the pillow case that I hung up at the end of my bed. It would certainly not fit into the stocking that was pinned to the chimney breast. Would he know where to leave it?

Christmas morning eventually arrived and I grabbed the stocking. I found some nuts, a sugar mouse and a little purse containing chocolate money. There was always a tangerine in the toe which filled the room with a strong orange perfume, because I always ate it straight away.

Then it was into my parent's room to open the pillow case that Santa had filled. I noticed that he had eaten the mince pie and drunk the glass of sherry that we had left out for him, so he must have got my note. But there was no sign of a bike, and I was very disappointed.

"Do you think Auntie will come?" I asked wistfully after I had opened my presents. I was beginning to miss her already.

"I suspect she will turn up when lunchtime comes and her tummy starts to rumble," said Dad. "She hates to be left out of anything so I expect, that come twelve o'clock, she will be knocking on the door as if nothing had happened."

Mum was less sympathetic. "Well, I'm not going to lay a place for her and I don't think we should answer the door," she exclaimed. "That will teach her a lesson. Feast of Beelzebub my foot! Your aunt has to learn she can't always have things her way. Cancelling Christmas! Whatever next?"

"Where is your Christmas spirit?" asked Dad. "It will be 'bah, humbug' next. I will have to call you Mrs Scrooge."

I pointed out that Aunt Lillian had not been at Midnight Mass.

"That was why it went without any mishap and we were home in bed before 1 a.m.," Mum retorted.

I knew that Mum had been dreading the service because it was usually interrupted by Aunt Lillian either singing loudly out of tune or moaning that things were not to her liking.

After breakfast we got ready to go off to church again. We were not usually a churchgoing family, but Christmas and Easter were special and we joined the congregation on those occasions. Funerals, christenings and weddings were attended throughout the year and I went to Sunday School, otherwise we left God to his own devices.

Noon arrived and the family started to gather. Still no sign of Aunt Lillian.

"I don't think she is going to turn up, you know," I said. "She would have been here by now if she was going to come. She didn't come to church this morning, either. She never misses the Christmas morning service."

Dad made light of it. "She has probably changed her religion again," he chuckled. "She could be a Buddhist or a Mormon or even a Jehovah's Witness."

"No, I think she has tried all of those and found them

wanting," Mum informed him. "I suspect all those churches were really pleased that she passed them over. I know, Mr Goss the Vicar, would be relieved if she gave his church a miss on a permanent basis too."

We were just about to sit down to lunch when there was a knock at the door. "See, I told you. There she is, dead on the dot," said Dad. "She must have smelt the turkey cooking."

I rushed to the door and flung it wide. Aunt Lillian was sitting on the door step with a big red spotted handkerchief held up to her eyes. She started wailing like a banshee and I jumped back in surprise. "What's the matter?" I yelled.

"You can well ask," she sniffed. "Ignored by my family and left out in the cold, starving hungry and neglected, that's what I am. Who would leave a poor old lady alone on a day like this? When I think of all I have done for this family − I am cut to the quick by the hard-heartedness of some people." She tried to stand up, but fell forward on her hands and knees.

Dad came to the door and asked: "Who is this we find here on the doorstep? Is it a tramp or Tiny Tim, or could it be the Little Goose Girl? No it is Lillian." He was laughing as he put out a hand to help her up. Her glasses were all askew and she hiccupped loudly before starting to giggle. The hat she was wearing was now at a jaunty angle, and she looked really funny sitting there in the snow.

"Oh, Lillian what have you been up to this time?" he enquired. "Have you been drinking?"

"Only a thimbleful of sherry to pick up my spirit, when I realised how unloved I am and how nobody had invited me to join in the family feast," she claimed.

"That was what you asked us to do," said Mother, who had joined us at the door. "So that was what we did. You are an adult and perfectly entitled to have your own opinion on the 'pagan rituals' that we are preparing, so we left you in peace. No Christmas cards, no presents and no feast, as requested."

Lillian refused to listen. "You just ignored a poor sick old woman and left her in a cold garret with only bread and water to eat." She started to cry again and blew her nose on the big spotted handkerchief, making a loud trumpeting noise.

"Don't exaggerate. You don't live in a garret and you certainly are not sick," Mum said quite acerbically. "Come in, if you are coming in, or close the door and let us get on with lunch." With that Mother returned to the kitchen.

"Is that any way to invite a guest to join you?" asked Lillian, staggering into the hall and almost falling over umbrellas in the hall stand. "Silly place to put umbrellas," she muttered. She pulled off her mackintosh and tried to hang it up, but kept missing the peg. Eventually she left it in a heap on the floor.

"I'm just going up to the toilet," she called. With that, she scrambled up the stairs on all fours like a cat on a hot tin roof.

We left her to it and all returned to the dining room when suddenly there was a whooping sound followed by a loud crash.

We ran out to find Aunt Lillian lying on the hall floor laughing gleefully. "I used to be able to slide down the banisters," she spluttered. "I'm not sure what happened this time."

"What happened was, you forgot how old you are," shouted Mum from the kitchen. "Fancy behaving like a child when you are nearing eighty. What will you think of next?"

"I dread to think," chuckled Dad as he picked Lillian up. "Come in quickly or lunch will be cold. We laid a place for you anyway. You see we didn't really forget you."

The only other mishap was, when Aunt Lillian tried to stab her peas and they flew all over the table like grapeshot fired from a rifle. This caused great hilarity. Her table manners left a lot to be desired on this occasion and we certainly kept her away from the sherry for the rest of the day.

We played the usual games and sang round the piano and a good time was had by all. Christmas was back to normal and it was the last we heard of the Feast of Beelzebub.

Oh, I forgot to mention. My bike was standing outside the back door with tinsel wound round the handlebars and a note attached which said: 'Sorry, I could not get this down the chimney! Love from Santa.'

# CHAPTER 17

# Testing Bank Security

"Are you ready?" Aunt Lillian called from the bedroom. "We need to go to the bank this morning."

"I have been ready for ages," I replied.

Lillian appeared in the doorway dressed in the leather jacket with the roaring tiger on the back that Trevor, my cousin, had loaned to her when she took the disastrous bike ride and landed up in the millpond. She was also carrying the bright yellow helmet under her arm. He had obviously never retrieved them. I suspect because he did not want to remind her that he still, according to her, owed her a trip on his motorbike.

"Why are you dressed like that? You haven't persuaded poor Trevor to take you on his bike again? Mum will be furious if she finds out you have blackmailed him into another trip. Anyway, I thought we were going to walk down to the library. Look, I have brought my books to change."

"I didn't blackmail him, as you put it. I just pointed out his obligations after he accepted the money from me for the repairs. That's not blackmail, that's just common and garden business sense." She drew herself up to her full five feet and looked me in the eye. "If you were older you would understand these things. We are going to the library after we have been to the bank. I just need to test something out, and no, Trevor is not taking me down there. We are going on 'Shanks's Pony'."

I had always wondered why it was called 'Shanks's Pony' and imagined us going into the village on a fat little pony and tying it up to the railings outside the Post Office.

"Then why are you dressed up like that? You can hardly move in that outfit and you might trip up and fall on your nose like you did last time." I could not help laughing at the memory of the pile up in the water and the crowds that gathered on the bank of the millpond that day to view the spectacle.

"I am not going to walk at all. You are going to push me," she retorted, dragging the trousers behind her.

"Why do I have to push you down the village, have you hurt yourself or something? I am not going to push you there in Wonkey Donkey you know." I could feel the panic starting when I thought of what people would say and how they would laugh at us.

"No, we are not taking Wonkey Donkey. I rescued a wheelchair from outside the cottage across the green. Old Mrs Daniels died last week you know and the family were throwing it away and so I asked if I could have it. I knew it would come in useful when I read the news in the papers this morning. Go and get it out of the shed and bring it to the back door and I will put these trousers on out on the step."

I ran over to the shed and sure enough there was an old fashioned wheelchair. I must admit that I was always more willing than most members of the family to take part in my aunt's madcap schemes, but even I was beginning to have my doubts about today's escapade, but my curiosity got the better of me. I pushed it up to the backdoor step where my aunt was struggling to stand up. The leathers were far too big for her and she really looked a sight attempting to stand upright holding on to the door jamb.

Turning to me she muttered: "We'll have to do something about you Jojo, you look just like yourself and that will never do at all."

"Of course I look like myself. Who did you expect me to look like?"

"As I said, it will never do. You need a disguise so that even your mother will not recognise you. Go and get my cape from the hallstand and also my black velour hat. That should do the trick."

For an eight year old I was quite small for my age so I knew that it would swamp me and come right down to the ground and I pointed this out to her.

"That's just what we need. Nobody will know who you are and I will put the helmet on with the visor down and everyone will think we are strangers from out of town."

I had the cape on, which did come right down to the

ground and the hat came down to rest on the top of my nose. I could only see the path for a few feet in front of me. "Well, is this what you want? I can't see a thing."

"Perfect," she enthused. "Off we go then. You push and I will steer you. It's not that far and I am as light as a feather so you will not have any problems pushing me all the way to the bank. After that I can take this outfit off and we can load it all onto the wheelchair and go to the library."

"Then why are we both dressed like this to go to the bank?" I asked.

"You'll see when we get there. I have been very worried about that bank and my suspicions were confirmed when I read this morning's paper. They mentioned that banks need to look at their security systems. So I need to test something because all my worldly wealth is tied up in that bank."

We arrived at the bank in one piece and I paused outside to catch my breath. "What next?"

She pulled a red spotted handkerchief out of her pocket and handed it to me. "Tie this round your face, then just push me in the door and follow my lead. Go on now, what are you waiting for? If you don't hurry they will close for lunch and we will not get to the library either and the opportunity will have been lost."

I had put the library books in the basket under the seat and grabbed them and said: "How about I go to the library whilst you go into the bank?"

"I can't do this by myself Jojo. I need your help. This is

a matter of national importance, so stop fiddling about and push me into the bank." With this, she pulled the visor down and in we went because I knew it was impossible to ignore her instructions without it causing a major uproar.

We clanged through the double swing doors to be confronted by a long queue at the counter and my aunt shouted in a deep voice that I hardly recognised: "Hands up, this is a bank raid!"

The Vicar turned to us, raised his hat and cheerily said: "Good morning Mrs Auger and how are you this bright morning? Hello Jojo I did not see you there. What are you up to?"

"I am not Mrs Auger, you have made a mistake. I am a cunning bank robber from out of town and this is my assistant. She has a gun under that cloak and you had better hand over the money this instance."

Everyone carried on as before. Totally ignoring us, the teller behind the counter called out: "Morning Mrs Auger. We won't be long and then we can deal with your query."

"I do not have a query. I am here to rob the bank. You should take your responsibilities seriously and worry about the safety of your customers and their money. It is this flippant attitude that banks have, that causes economic chaos in the world. "

"Yes, Mrs Auger, I am sure you are right but I have to get on and serve all these people before I can get to you and deal with your bank robbery," said the bank clerk quite wearily. He had had dealings with my aunt before and knew that there was no point in trying to argue with her.

I could feel that my aunt was getting quite angry at being recognised by all and sundry and not taken seriously.

"What is the date today?" somebody called out, "is it the 1st April? This looks like an April Fool's joke to me or perhaps it is Candid Camera. It could be our fifteen minutes of fame and we will all make the headlines in the local paper. Where are the cameras?"

Suddenly I noticed that our local Bobby was at the front of the queue and I pointed this out to my aunt. "Psst! PC Mark is over there and he will arrest us and I don't fancy going to jail and I know Mum will be furious when she finds out that I took part in a bank raid and am not home in time for lunch. She has made Egg and Cheese Pie today and that's my favourite."

"Don't chicken out now, Jojo," she whispered to me. "We have to find out how good the security is in this bank. If I find it is no good, I am going to test all the banks in the village and then decide where to put my money in the future. Banks are getting lax these days and not looking after the pennies, so how can we expect them to look after the pounds."

From the corner of my eye I saw PC Mark step towards us. "What's going on here?" he said in a very gruff voice. "Is this a bank robbery? I'll just have to take these two villains into custody and they will go up before the beak next week. A few days in the slammer will soon break their spirits. They will probably get twenty years or more."

I swallowed hard. I didn't want to spend twenty years in jail. "Hello, PC Mark, it's me, Jojo," I said tentatively as I pulled the handkerchief down and looked up at him. "You know me, I am Jojo from Bradbourne Road and I go to St. Mary's Primary School in the village and I sit next to Colin. You know him, he is your son."

He glared down at me. "I don't think you are really Jojo. I think you are that desperado Pete the Bandit, that I read about at the station this morning. There is a price on his head and he goes around with a partner in a wheelchair and I think I will claim the reward when I hand you two over."

"No, really PC Mark, I am Jojo and this is my Aunt Lillian. You know her as well. All the people here know my aunt." I looked around desperately. "You do know us, don't you?"

"No," they all chorused. They looked at me blankly as though they had never seen me before.

I was panicking and didn't know what to do when Mrs Kelsey, the butcher's wife added: "We've never seen them before but we did read about them in the local paper and we were warned that they could be dangerous. Take them away now and save us all."

I was cowering behind the wheelchair feeling a little desperate. "Tell them Aunty, please!"

"I don't know what you mean. I'm not your aunt; I am the most successful bank robber in the county. Nobody has been able to catch me." With that she jumped up and fell over because the legs of the leathers had quickly reverted to their original size and she landed on the floor like a stranded Michelin Man. She thrashed around for a while unable to get up.

"Isn't somebody going to help me?" she gasped. "I can't get up."

PC Mark walked over to her, pulled her upright and yanked the helmet off her head. "Well, if it isn't Mrs Auger. What do you think you are doing encouraging your niece into a life of crime? You should be ashamed of yourself at your age, and anyway, what are you doing trying to rob this bank?"

Aunt Lillian grinned at him a little sheepishly. "Well, it is like this officer. I read in this morning's papers that the security in banks is not what it should be and this bank is supposed to be looking after my money and so I thought I should test out their systems. I must say that they leave a lot to be desired, if you ask me."

A shout came from the back of the queue which now went out of the door: "Can we get moving please, I want to get back to work and haven't got all day to wait here whilst a silly old woman decides to play at bank robbers."

My aunt took umbrage to this remark and snapped back: "Who are you calling a silly old woman? I have done you all a favour by pointing out the flaws in the system and you should be grateful to me. They will have to tighten up their security now."

She was squirming trying to get her hands out of the sleeves. "Jojo, come over here and help me with the zip."

Someone else in the queue muttered: "I think the whole village is grateful to you Mrs Auger because you always make us laugh and give us something to talk about. At least we appreciate that."

I felt a bit better as I saw that some of the people were smiling at us and PC Mark had walked away and gone back to his place in the queue. Perhaps we would avoid twenty years in jail after all. With some difficulty I managed to get her out of the outfit and we piled it all on the seat of the wheelchair and left.

"Shall we join the queue?" I asked.

"No, I don't need anything from here today. I just wanted to test them and I have done that, so let's go to the library." With that we left the bank pushing the loaded wheelchair in front of us.

I must say that my aunt is the only person I know who can leave the scene of chaos that she has caused with her head held high and no sense of embarrassment. To her it was a job well done.

Today she would have been declared insane and put away, but then she was seen as a true eccentric and in those days we were proud of true eccentrics and let them be.

# CHAPTER 18

# A Hot Line to God

"Hurry up, Jojo, I want to speak to God," Aunt Lillian urged one morning as we made our way down the High Street. She went on: "He has got several things wrong when it comes to design and I have decided to help him put them right. More people would go to church then. There is not much point in going if you know he makes mistakes. The church was half empty last week when I popped in for morning service. So I am going to help him out of the pickle he seems to have got himself into."

We were approaching St. Mary's at this point and Aunt Lillian began to drag me towards the door, because I was resisting quite forcefully. I had been there before when she had given God a piece of her mind and I did not want to have to listen to it again. It was so embarrassing seeing my eccentric aunt being thrown out by the Vicar for berating the crucified Christ that stood above the altar.

"I don't want to go in there," I wailed. "Remember what the Vicar said last time. You'll get banned."

"How can he ban me?" she demanded to know. "It is a public building and it is not only church people who can talk to God, you know. Anyone can talk to him at any time and I just want to put him straight on a couple of points. No harm in that, is there?"

I was still recovering from the mortification of when Aunt Lillian had denounced the Vicar as a hypocrite for telling her that she could not bring a dog into morning prayers. Pegotty was a scruffy little mongrel she took with her when the mood was upon her. She felt strongly that animals, as a part of God's creation, should be allowed to participate in the service and she told the Vicar so in no uncertain terms.

In the past she had been banned from St. John's up the High Street for the very same reason, only that time it was her ducks. On that occasion a loud altercation ensued which was joined by various members of the congregation. Some were in favour of animals being allowed in and some were very much against it. Others just wanted to stir things up to alleviate the boredom of attending morning service before sneaking off to the local for a pre-lunch pint.

Never one to back down in an argument, Aunt Lillian demanded that the parishioners stage a sit-in to protest at the treatment Pegotty had received. She felt she was offended and upset by this rejection by one of God's chosen. Aunt Lillian and Pegotty were not going to budge and she told the Vicar that he should start the service immediately as he was holding up proceedings and she had to get home because she had left the roast in the oven.

The morning service had deteriorated into a near riot,

with several voices raised, and it had almost come to fisticuffs; it surely would have done if PC Mark, who had been sitting near the back, had not taken some action. He mounted the pulpit and shouted for silence.

Quiet descended and the worshipers meekly took their seats, looking very ashamed of themselves for their outburst. The constable called the Vicar forward and ordered him to carry on with the first hymn, so the organ struck up, quite appropriately, with the first chords of 'Fight the Good Fight'.

Pegotty had ignored the fray and was sitting quietly in the front row being patted by a self-satisfied Lillian, who sat with her hymn book open ready to worship her Lord, as if butter would not melt in her mouth.

I was remembering this as we reached the door of St. Mary's. This was the temporary church, which looked somewhat like a Nissan hut, that had been constructed in the grounds of the bombed out building and was not one of my aunt's favourites. She had protested that it should have been returned to its former Gothic splendour but was duly informed that there were not the necessary funds at the present time.

"Come on, Jojo. Hurry yourself, we can't keep God waiting. He hasn't got all day, you know."

I gave up as I knew there was no point in arguing and, without further ado, I followed my aunt up the main aisle. She stood at the bottom of the steps gazing up at Christ on the cross.

"You can sit over there out of the way, while I have a private word with God," she said, pointing to the front row of chairs.

"Can't I go and wait outside?" I asked tentatively.

"No, you can't," Aunt Lillian insisted, putting a stray grey hair back in place. "You need to learn to talk to God when you get older and you want things put right. It is never too early to learn new skills, and talking to God is one of them. There is a right way and a wrong way to do it."

"Excuse me, sir," she began. Then, looking over her shoulder at me, she said: "You must always show respect when you talk to God."

She turned back. "Now where was I? Oh, yes. I thought I should come here and tell you about a couple of faults in your designs. You can then put them right and perhaps more people will come to church. I have made a note so that I don't forget anything." With this she pulled out what looked like a rather long list of things to discuss. "Firstly, it is finger nails. They are always breaking or need cutting and they are a nuisance.

"Then there is hair. This causes me problems as I have to pay good money to go to the hairdressers. If you could see your way to giving me a stylish cut which would always stay the same I could save a fortune."

She paused as if waiting for a reply to her request. When a little time had elapsed she carried on. "Illness is a bit of a nuisance and if you have made us all in your image, I would have thought you could have got rid of that inconvenience.

"Whilst you are thinking about it; old age is a bind and you might have sorted that out better. I am not sure you have been thinking in the long term. We humans have to put up with quite a lot you know."

She again waited but no reply came. "Lastly," she opined in a strange voice, "these are definitely a problem."

I realised that she had taken out her false teeth and was waving them up towards the figure of Christ. "Firstly, you get a set as a child and they fall out of their own accord and then these adult ones decay and need replacing. False teeth would not have been needed if you had thought about the initial design a little more carefully."

"Urgh, Auntie. Don't do that," I shrieked. I hated her false teeth and I always shut my eyes when I went into the bathroom in the morning because often this pair of teeth seemed to be grinning at me from the bottom of the glass where she left them overnight.

It was difficult to understand what my aunt was saying when she removed her teeth. Now she was mumbling while looking up to the cross: "Sharks have more than 3,000 teeth you know, and when one comes out the others move forward to fill the gap. So why haven't you organised it that humans grow new teeth that move forward to replace the old ones. If it's good enough for sharks, then surely it should be good enough for the descendants of Adam and Eve?"

I was quite impressed by the way she was giving God a piece of her mind. Most of her points seemed to have merit and I wondered why nobody else had thought of speaking directly to Him.

As nothing bad had happened so far, I plucked up the courage to say: "Could you ask him to make me really clever and then I would not have to waste time going to school? I hate maths and I am not very good at PE."

"Hush, child," scolded by aunt. "Do you think God has nothing better to do than worry about making you clever? He is a busy man and has so many important people to listen to – like the Pope or the Archbishop of Canterbury. He can't listen to children as well. They should be seen and not heard."

"But Jesus said that little children should be brought to him," I protested. "Won't he listen to them when they see him?" I had read about that in the Bible and had imagined myself talking to Jesus, but there was not much point if he was not going to listen to me.

"Of course, Jesus will listen to children – that's his job," Aunt Lillian conceded. "But I am talking to God, and that is just for adults."

She seemed rather pleased with herself until I found a flaw in her argument: "So why were you looking at Jesus on the cross when you were talking just then?"

"You really do ask too many questions," my aunt replied somewhat waspishly. "I am just facing towards Jesus, but I am really speaking to God."

She then carried on with her requests. "Whilst I am here, God, can you do something about the Vicar's wife? She had me banned from the WVS coffee mornings, and a free cup of coffee never goes amiss. I am also pretty sure she is lobbying to get me thrown out of the WI as well. She needs teaching a lesson because she is getting somewhat above her station, you know. I was only telling the truth when I said she was a gossip monger and that she should wash her mouth out with carbolic soap for spreading lies about me."

Lillian never saw the mote in her own eye and I was beginning to worry that God might be getting a bit fed up with all this criticism. I did not want him to get angry and send a flood – like he did when poor Noah crossed the line.

"Don't you think we should go home now?" I asked tentatively.

"No. I have not finished yet," my aunt insisted. "There are a lot more things I need to speak to God about. He doesn't always have time to listen, and now I have his ear I think it would be best to sort everything out in one go. If you stop interrupting I can get on with it."

I tried a new tack by revealing: "My tummy is rumbling and I think that is a bit rude if God is listening."

"I have just told you that God does not listen to children, so you are all right." My aunt swivelled round again. "Are you still listening God? I think that it should rain at night between the hours of midnight and five in the morning because it is so inconvenient to hold an umbrella when carrying shopping. I don't suppose you realised that we need three hands to do that, and you have only supplied us with two."

I began to giggle, imagining us with three hands, and wondering whether the extra one would be at the front or back of our bodies. If it was at the back we would have to alter all our clothes to accommodate this new appendage, and I bet Aunt Lillian had not thought of the expense of that.

At this point I realised it was getting quite dark in the unlit church. When we had entered the sun was shining through the stained glass window and made wonderful patterns on the floor, but now the building looked gloomy and quite menacing.

I heard Aunt Lillian say: "Well, God, I hope that you have written these points on your 'things to do list' so that you don't forget them. I will check back with you later in the week and I am sure I will find some more things that need sorting out."

I noticed that she had adopted her 'school teacher' voice, and I was beginning to feel that God might not like her lecturing him in this manner.

At that moment there was a flash of light, an almighty crash and the building shook. We both jumped up and looked around us. I was really frightened and grabbed hold of Aunt Lillian's hand.

"Let's go now," I stammered, pulling her towards the door.

"Yes, we had better leave," agreed Lillian in a trembling voice. "Perhaps I have said too much. I really thought God would be more understanding."

We rushed to the door and out into the pouring rain.

"Do you think it is going to rain for forty days and forty nights?" I asked, looking up at the black sky. It was certainly raining cats and dogs.

"Well, if this keeps up perhaps I'll ask your uncle to

think about building an ark," chuckled Aunt Lillian as she put up her umbrella. I noticed that she had recovered her usual sense of humour.

# Looking Back Through Rose Tinted Glasses

# Looking Back Through Rose Tinted Glasses

Now that I have reached a ripe old age myself, I can look back with fond memories to the time spent with my eccentric aunt, who was a unique and very special person. The stories were based on my personal recollections and I have left most members of the family out of these tales. Aunt Lillian was married for over forty five years to a very patient and quiet man and my brother steered well clear of her most of the time, whilst I loved being part of her escapades.

After the grim years of the war, everyone was looking for a spark of joy and something to bring a smile back to the face of the world. My Great Aunt Lillian certainly gave our village something to laugh about and her antics were discussed by all and sundry.

It was a more innocent time and people were more accepting of the foibles of others. Health and Safety rules did not apply, while Social Services did not exist. And the local bobby upheld law and order in a friendly manner, with a few quiet words to ensure that any embarrassing episodes were forgiven, if not forgotten. Children who

scrumped apples were given a stern talking to or a cuff round the ear and sent on their way with the warning "I will tell your dad if I catch you again."

Bank managers knew their customers by name and the villagers all looked out for each other. Life moved at a slower pace. There were no televisions or computer games, and little of the hustle and bustle of the big city encroached into the lives of the people of our community.

Hindsight allows me to see why my mother found Aunt Lillian such an embarrassment – somebody to be avoided if possible. As I revealed earlier, my mother would often pull me into a shop when she saw Aunt Lillian in the High Street, just to avoid having to meet up with her. Living in a small village and being constantly reminded of her escapades must have been awful for my prim and proper mother, but the rose tinted glasses that I saw her through made her a magical person for a child to be with.

She had a great appetite for life and her imagination helped me to have big ambitions. She always told me to dream big; wishing for small things was a waste of a wish. She encouraged me to see the world through her eyes and be optimistic of the future.

I still step carefully into a ring of toadstools, and say "Good Morning, Mr. Magpie, and how is your wife?" when one of those birds crosses my path. I continue to cross my fingers when going under ladders, and say "Hares, hares, hares – rabbits, rabbits, rabbits" on the first day of the month.

Aunt Lillian was a drama queen who loved the attention that my mother shunned. She wanted to be noticed and enjoyed every minute of her long life. I often wonder how God got on when he eventually plucked up the courage to call her to him. I suspect he may have had second thoughts.

As I grew up, things changed and the pace of the world increased. Aunt Lillian moved to Wales to live near her daughter. She bought a big mobile home which had two bedrooms, a large kitchen-diner and large sitting room. The bathroom was plumbed in, with a full sized bath in it. It was a bungalow really, albeit a bungalow on wheels.

I remember visiting her on one occasion to find that the bathroom was spattered with black paint and the room was very dark. When I asked her why it was so dark, she informed me that while lying in the bath she had suddenly seen a plane that had just taken off from Cardiff airport. She told me it was then that she realised people in the plane would be able to see her naked, and she couldn't stand for that, so she had painted over the skylight. She had such an imagination. She was stick thin and just five foot tall and you could have missed seeing her from 100 feet away, let alone from an airliner accelerating up into the sky.

Whenever I recounted her adventures to my friends, which I have to admit I sometimes exaggerated, they always told me to write them down. So I did, and I hope that you have enjoyed reading them as much as I have enjoyed recalling my childhood spent with such a special person.

I might have to apologise to her, if we should ever meet in the afterlife, as I have taken some liberties with the truth and have exaggerated some of her escapades but I know that deep down she would be pleased with the fact that I have used the imagination that she created in me and would be proud of the way I have portrayed her. As she said: "Never spoil a good story for the truth!"

I now write articles for magazines and edit an online magazine called www.giddylimits.co.uk which has enabled me to further my writing ambitions. I have also created children's stories which I read in my local primary school and I hope to publish at a later date.

I am a member of the Society of Women Writers and Journalists and the International Travel Writers' Alliance.

Life has been very good to me and I can attribute so much to having known Great Aunt Lillian. The world will never see the like of her again and that really is a pity and all I can say is "Oh My Giddy Aunt!"

# Acknowledgements

Firstly I would like to thank Gerry Granshaw, my close friend and business partner on www.giddylimits.co.uk, for all her encouragement and help with the writing of this book. Without her support I would never have never written *Oh My Giddy Aunt!*

I would also like to thank Tony Flood who patiently edited this book. He is an author himself, so fully appreciates the difficulties I encountered. Find out more about Tony Flood by visiting:
www.fantasyadventurebooks.com/ and:
www.celebritiesconfessions.com/

My eternal gratitude goes to my fantastic friend Erika Eadie, who proofread my stories and guided me through the use of the colon and semi-colon.

Finally, to Garry Davies who drew the cartoons and front cover and has fully captured the essence of Aunt Lillian and Jojo. Thank You. He can be contacted on garry.davies657@tiscali.co.uk